PREDATOR IN THE LANES

A VIKING WITCH MYSTERY

CATE MARTIN

Cover design by Shezaad Sudar.

Rune art by BettyStrange at Dreamstime.com.

Ratatoskr Press logo by Aidan Vincent Kise.

ISBN 978-1-965167-01-4

❋ Formatted with Vellum

CHAPTER ONE

AFTER THE BRUTAL heat of early August, followed by the furious intensity of an epic hailstorm that quickly shifted back into a smothering atmosphere of heat and humidity, September was a real blessing.

The sun had risen over Lake Superior on the first of the month, speckling the surface of the iron gray lake with rosy-gold sparkles of light, to gently warm the refreshingly brisk morning air. A soft rain had fallen the night before, but not so much as to leave muddy puddles all over the cobblestoned roads of Villmark.

Or, for that matter, all over the lakeside town of Runde. Because while I lived in Villmark—the village of descendants from a lost Viking tribe that had settled on the shore of Lake Superior long before the days of Christopher Columbus—I also spent as much time as I could in the more conventional northern Minnesotan town of Runde. Especially now that my grandmother's cabin was finally finished, and she had moved out of the rental mobile home in the parking lot of the municipal building.

The municipal building that she used her magic to turn into an authentic Viking era mead hall after sunset every day.

Yeah, I know. My life is a lot. But I'm used to it. Half of my friends wear swords while patrolling the borders of Villmark to keep the likes of trolls, giants and other monsters at bay, and the other half are waiting tables in the busy diner off the highway, or long haul trucking to the coast and back, or running their own café/bookstore business.

And I float between both worlds.

Although the more my grandmother had sunk her roots into only Runde these days, the more I found myself compensating by rooting deeper down into Villmark.

But while a magical barrier protected Villmark from being discovered by the outside world, the weather permeated both sides of that barrier. The hailstorm that pelted one pelted the other.

And the bright sunshine that bathed one bathed the other in equally golden, warm tones.

So far, this September had been exceptionally nice. It had been warm enough to go out without a jacket, but never so hot that walking to the market was all that was needed to break out into a sweat.

And, as if that perfect day had been some sort of template, every day in September after that had been a pasted copy of the first. A gentle rain on occasion, but only at night and never more than a shimmering wetness to the grass and trees left by dawn.

Those trees weren't turning colors just yet. That wouldn't start really happening until October. But after the drought of late summer, the trees were a dappled pattern of green and gold that made the hills look like they were dancing with even the softest of breezes.

And the sky was an almost Mediterranean shade of indigo blue.

So it might have seemed ironic to an impartial observer that, while Esja assisted Roarr with the intricacies of watercolors as their works in progress gained layer after layer of bright color, my own drawing pad on the easel in front of me was all the black of ink on the matte white of my thickest paper.

But only if that observer didn't know me or my art particularly well. Because as much as I was decently skilled with any art media, my two greatest loves were always charcoal and ink. And those media encouraged chiaroscuro.

Which usually I liked. I love bold contrasts between light and dark and always lean into it with all my work, whether magical or purely artistic. And, being a volva—a Norse witch—in training as well as an aspiring book illustrator, I had plenty of opportunities for both pursuits.

I suppose the fact that I was doing such stark work while facing a gorgeous view of blue skies, green and gold trees, and all the bright colors of the homes of Villmark spread out over the hillside south of my floor-to-ceiling windows in my great room might have been ironic.

But, on the other hand, it felt all too appropriate to me. Because while I knew on a surface level that this run of fine weather and the beauty of the view I woke to every morning were some of life's best little miracles, I couldn't quite feel it. Not deep down inside.

It had been two months now since my boyfriend Thorbjorn had gone north with Esja's brother, my close friend Loke. And it had been a month since my magic cat, Mjolner, had been able to find them.

And that break in contact—as tenuous as it had always been since Mjolner couldn't actually talk to me to let me know how the two of them were doing—was making it hard to see the bright colors of autumn in Villmark.

Or to appreciate the smells of the apples that everyone was baking with at the moment.

Or to bask in the touch of the breezes that were always refreshing without ever being chilling.

Winter was coming. This fine weather would end. And what a crime it would be if I never once appreciated it while it was here.

And yet... I just couldn't.

"I don't get it," Roarr said to Esja with a sigh as he sat back to look at the muddy tones of the paper mounted on his easel. "Yours looks so much nicer than mine."

The two of them were painting the same landscape, but I was, as usual, focused on the latest rune in my ongoing studies with the old wise man Haraldr. This one was naudhr, the rune of need. It looked like two sticks, one vertical and the other at a cross angle, like when someone used just that friction to start a fire.

An arduous process, almost as arduous as my attempt to connect to the concept it was supposed to invoke.

The only need I could focus on was my bone-deep longing to see Thorbjorn and Loke again.

But Roarr's words were a welcome break to my feeble attempts at proper concentration. I set aside my ink brush and stood up to stretch my back before walking over to stand between their two easels.

He wasn't wrong. Her landscape was delicate, her use of color subtle but confident. But, to be fair, Esja had been painting almost since birth. And while she did some sketching, most of her work had been focused entirely on watercolors. She could do things with those paints that I struggled to replicate, and I had graduated from a rigorous art school.

I looked at his attempt at the landscape we were all facing, then looked over at Esja's. I could see the problem at once, beyond just the varying levels of skill.

But I was trying to encourage Esja to take on the role of teacher, so I said nothing. Even though she was casting nervous looks my way, waiting for me to jump in. I remained silent.

"I think you forgot some of the things I told you about mixing colors," Esja said at last. She was still looking to me for confirmation, but I kept my face impassive.

"I was cleaning my brush thoroughly before changing colors," Roarr said. Then he looked down at his large hands, covered all over in streaks of paint that he hadn't been cleaning as thoroughly from his own skin.

But that wasn't his problem.

"Look how much of your black and white has already been used up," Esja said. "I told you to use those sparingly."

"I did," he said defensively. But we were all looking at the evidence even as he said those words. "I mean, I tried to. I guess I don't get it. If I see where the leaves over here are a lighter green, don't I use white to make it lighter?"

"You could make a paler green that way, but what you're looking at isn't really just a whiter shade of green," Esja said. She pointed out the window towards the trees in question. "Look more carefully at it. Really look. Just focus on the green."

"Okay," Roarr said, looking out the window with his eyes squinted almost shut as he focused on just the green.

"They aren't whiter, the lighter patches, are they?" she said. "The green is lighter, but it's reflecting a lot of the yellow from the other leaves around it. Not white."

"Okay," Roarr said, but skeptically. He wasn't sure if she was pulling his leg.

But then something clicked inside his head, and I watched as his eyes started darting around all over that hillside. "Okay, so the yellow leaves that look darker are kind of green in the same way?"

"Definitely not blacker," Esja said. "The black is what's making your final picture so muddy. Blacks and whites really take over a painting when you use them even a little bit too much. They overwhelm. You really have to look carefully and focus on the colors you're actually seeing. Like the way those yellows and greens reflect each other."

Roarr just nodded thoughtfully.

But I stepped away before either of them could see the emotion I knew was coloring my cheeks.

I felt like Esja had just given me a thorough dressing down on my attitude, and she hadn't even been talking to me. Not even obliquely.

And yet, I could see she was right. I wasn't looking well enough. Art was one thing, but I was letting the blacks and whites dominate in my life as well. And they weren't exactly working for me in the moment.

"Do you want to try again?" Esja asked Roarr.

"Maybe later," he said. "It's getting late. And Nora is serving cinnamon buns with the first barrel of her hard cider at the mead hall tonight. That and a little roast chicken and root vegetables? Well worth getting there early for."

I couldn't argue with that. Nora, my grandmother, had been expanding her menu down at the mead hall. It was like, now that she wasn't managing the contractors who had built her cabin back from scratch after I had accidentally flattened her old one with a magical tornado, she needed something else to fill her time.

Or maybe, now that I was taking on more and more of the duties of volva that had always been hers alone before, she just had the time to focus on the mead hall that she had always longed for.

Or maybe a bit of both.

It was nice to see, and I could feel her exhausted happiness every time I stopped in to see her.

And Roarr wasn't wrong. Roast chicken and root vegetables with all the fresh herbs from my grandmother's thriving garden sounded so good my mouth watered just at the thought. And mulled cider with cinnamon buns felt like autumn perfection.

And it would be a chance to see my Runde friends again. In Villmark, I tended to lose track of the days, but I was pretty sure it was the weekend in Runde. Andrew and Jessica would be at the mead hall for sure, and Michelle and her new boyfriend Kristofer as well, if he was in town and not out driving his truck.

"Ingrid?" Esja said, and I realized they had both been looking at me. Like they were waiting for permission.

"You guys go ahead," I said as I moved back to my easel. The page was covered with renditions of the naudhr rune that ranged from the most basic slashing strokes to an elaborate version that would make any illuminator from the Middle Ages sick with envy.

"You're still blocked with that rune?" Esja asked.

"Surely an evening off would help?" Roarr put in.

"Or doing the opposite of drawing it over and over again," Esja said. "Like… dancing."

I just bit back a laugh. I knew she was trying to be helpful, but Esja's answer to most of life's problems these days was dancing.

And having indulged her more than once, I had to admit, there was something to be said to letting the mind go and just moving your body around to an infectious beat.

But not that night. "No, you guys go ahead without me," I said. "I'll try to catch up later if I can, but no promises."

"You're not going to sit here and stew again, are you?" Esja asked.

Then she seemed to realize she had used the word "again" and blushed furiously.

But, that was fair. I *had* been stewing. A lot. And fruitlessly.

"No, I just want to catch Haraldr before he goes to bed and talk to him about things," I said. "I'm sure I'll be down soon enough. Unless I need to sleep on the problem. Sometimes that helps."

"Don't worry about us," Roarr said, even going so far as to grasp my wrist in his rough hand, if only fleetingly. He wasn't normally a touchy-feely person, but I didn't miss what he was really telling me.

He had said "us," but he had meant "Esja." I didn't need to worry about Esja. Because he would keep an eye out for her.

And although she hadn't had a single strange episode since we had brought her back to Villmark the month before, neither Roarr nor I were ready to relax our vigilance.

Some strange entity was far too interested in Esja, and far too capable of just sliding into her mind and making trouble. And while my grandmother had started teaching her some basic protective magic, she was making progress with it at about the rate that Roarr was mastering watercolors.

Still, it was a short walk from Villmark to Runde. And in Runde, she'd be close by my grandmother, inside the protection of all the spells I had helped my grandmother weave to protect that space. Esja would be safer there than she was even in my company.

She would be fine.

"Thank you," I said to Roarr.

We walked together out the front gate of my house, but parted ways there. As they headed north towards the commons, I could just catch Esja's words cajoling Roarr into dancing with her for just one song. He was refusing firmly enough, but somehow I was sure by the time they reached my grandmother's mead hall, he'd be talked into three dances and only one of them could be a slow song.

I smiled to myself as I headed south, past the marketplace to the public gardens that bordered Haraldr's house.

On the way, I tried really hard to appreciate the colors.

And I blamed the coming twilight for how muted everything still felt to me.

CHAPTER TWO

THE MARKETPLACE WAS CLOSING up for the night as I walked past it, but I lingered a bit in the public gardens. The largest part of these gardens are orchards of fruit trees and raised beds of herbs, both culinary and medicinal. And the greenhouse at the back of the gardens was filled with even more, and rarer plants.

But I made the most of the last dying light of the sun to take a quick stroll through what was, in the summertime, the flower gardens.

I've always liked the way gardens look in the fall, the way the flowers and greenery dry into ghostly versions of their summer selves. Everything is so delicate, crumbling at the softest brush of a fingertip. But that crumbling touch also released the last of the dying bloom's scent. I was never a goth girl—which kind of made me stand out in some of my art school classes, let me tell you—but this fading beauty always struck me on a deep level.

And, strangely, by the time it was too dark for me to make out more than the outlines of the plants around me, I felt better.

I mean, I still missed Thorbjorn. And Loke.

But now their absence felt more like a temporary thing. Like the dying of the flowers, it was just part of the wheel of life. And that wheel was always turning.

The flowers would bloom again, when spring came.

And I'd see Thorbjorn and Loke again. In due time.

Meanwhile, I had to get to Haraldr's house if I still wanted to catch him before bedtime. His bedtime, anyway.

It was a short walk past the grand Viking era timber longhouse that was the council hall to the more modern Scandinavian design of Haraldr's house. I climbed onto his porch, saw the light from his kitchen spilling in an elongated rectangle across the garden to the left of the house, and knocked on the door.

I wasn't surprised to see Fulla answer the door, although she seemed to grow a couple more inches every time I saw her. She was an orphan who lived in Haraldr's house to help him manage his household.

But I *was* surprised to see that she wasn't alone. There was another girl of about the same age of early teens standing beside her. And both of their faces were rosily glowing, as if I had just caught them mid giggling fit.

"Hello," I said.

"Hello, Ingrid," Fulla said, clearly pulling herself together to fulfill her role as Haraldr's assistant. She stepped back and held the door open so I could step into the mudroom. "This is my friend Brana. Brana, this is Ingrid Torfudottir."

"I know that," Brana whispered to her friend. But then she smiled up at me nervously. "Well met, volva."

"Well met, Brana," I said. They were both dressed in the traditional Villmarker girl clothes of an apron dress over a sheath-like dress, white linen over blue linen. And their blonde hair fell in long braids down their backs, although Fulla's hair was considerably thicker than her friend's.

But both of them had little butterfly clips in their hair. Just cheap plastic in pastel colors covered in glitter, the sort of thing I used to buy in a kiosk in a mall when I was their age.

Although where these two had gotten them, I had no idea. I

doubted either of them had ever been outside the borders of Villmark even to go down into Runde. Which, being a fishing village really, had no mall.

Still, things from the outside world just had a way of finding their way into Villmark, even into the hands of children. The isolationists hated it; they would prefer the children of Villmark had only proper Villmarker things and no knowledge of the greater world at all.

But ribbons, while fine in their own right, would never really be able to compete with glittery butterflies with bright—if fake—jewels for eyes.

"I don't think Haraldr was expecting you?" Fulla said with a puzzled frown.

"No, we don't have an appointment," I said. "I just wanted to talk with him, if he's available."

"He went into his library after dinner," Fulla said. "Brana was helping me with the dishes, but we were going to head to my room now. Unless you needed me?"

Far be it from me to get between a thirteen-year-old girl and whatever she wanted to get up to in her bedroom with her best friend. "No, I can find my own way. Thanks."

Fulla gave me a big, grateful smile. Then she and Brana scampered down the hall past the door to the kitchen to, presumably, her own room. They almost got the door closed behind them before erupting into giggles again.

The door to the library was closed, but there was light coming from underneath it. Firelight, but also lamplight. I knocked, then let myself inside.

As I had expected, Haraldr was tucked in his chair by the fire, a lap blanket drawn over his legs and a book open on his lap. And he was indeed attempting to get up as I came in, but settled gratefully back into his seat at my gesture.

"Ingrid. Well met," he said.

"I hope I'm not stopping by too late," I said.

"No, no," he said, readjusting the folds of the shawl that had slipped from his shoulders when he had started to get up from his chair. "I'm afraid I napped too excessively this afternoon, and sleep is bound to elude me for some hours now. And the book I chose to while away the time isn't grabbing my attention. I welcome whatever distraction you've come to offer me. I suppose this is about naudhr?"

"It feels appropriate, doesn't it?" I said as I settled into my customary chair across from his. "I mean, this rune represents resistance to will and action. So if it's fighting me..."

I trailed off with a shrug.

"You feel like it's fighting you?" he asked.

"Yeah," I said, but there was something in his tone that told me he didn't think that was true. "What do you think? That I'm fighting myself?"

"I wasn't thinking that, but apparently you were," he said with a spark of laughter in his eyes. "No, what I was thinking was what I'm always thinking when you come to see me."

"And what's that?" I asked.

"That you are always in such a hurry," he said. "The knowledge of the ages, knowledge our ancestors put together over generations and generations, and you want to learn it all at once. Learn it, master it, use it, all in a snap."

"It's not my ego," I said defensively. "It's necessity. Something is coming, and I have to be ready."

"Necessity," Haraldr said with a sly grin.

"Right. Naudhr," I said. "Maybe I understand this already better than I think I do."

Haraldr shrugged noncommittally. "I think you are progressing just as you should be, and in the proper time," he said. "All I would suggest you change is your approach. Your frame of mind."

"How so?" I asked.

"Just as the rune is trying to teach you," Haraldr said. "Circumstances are creating necessities for you, as you said. You need skills to be prepared, and you feel that need deeply."

"So, what do I have to change?" I asked. Because if he thought I was seeing where he was going, I really wasn't.

"You need more patience," he said. "The things you can't change, they are creating your necessities. Something is coming to Villmark, and you know you have to be prepared to face it. That is a necessity for you. You know the two men you rely on the most are gone from you and may remain so for some time. So you are on your own, if just for a time. That's a necessity."

"Patience isn't going to change any of that," I said.

"*Nothing* is going to change any of that," Haraldr said firmly. "Your patience is only in your reaction to those things. You need to find your way to working with the things you can't change. Because you'll never succeed in trying to work against them."

"What's the point of anything if I can't change things?" I asked, throwing up my hands in frustration.

"You can't change the past, can you?" he asked me mildly.

"Obviously not," I said. Although I had gone to the past once. And I wasn't convinced that changing it was impossible. Just that it was almost definitely a really bad idea to try.

"The past creates the restrictions that carry on into the future," he said. At my blank look, he leaned forward in his chair as if being closer would help me understand him more. "Thorbjorn went into the north and hasn't returned yet. That was in the past, and it will carry on into the future that you are, for some time, without him. You can't change that."

"I could go find him," I said.

He sat back and gave me a long, level look.

"I could," I said, when he carried on not speaking.

"He went north for a reason," Haraldr said. "And he went without you for a reason. Do you not trust his reasoning?"

"No, it's not that," I said, but in a slow drawl.

But if he heard my hesitation, he ignored it. "Trust him. Honor his choices. Be patient."

Now it was my turn to say nothing. But I did chew at my lip pretty aggressively.

"In the meantime," Haraldr said with a kind smile, "focus on what necessity is forging in you. Staying strong in this moment, that is building the will—the magical might—in you that you will need in the future. When Thorbjorn returns, if not sooner."

"Future," I said musingly. "Skuld."

"She is the Norn associated with this rune, yes," Haraldr said. "But I caution you again not to bring your understanding of the fates and karmas of other cultures to this area. The Norns and the well they use to tend the World Tree are not the fates with their spinning, weaving and cutting of threads. The Norns cut the wood to measure our days, but it is as a parent measures a child by making a mark in a doorway. It's a measure of what is, not a determination of what will be. The child is as tall as the child is. And so are the lengths of our lives. Skuld measures, but she doesn't determine."

"Okay," I sighed. "But I'm still worried. Esja has been perfectly fine since Roarr and I brought her back from that village in the north. And I don't know if what was inside of her at that well was actually some part of the Norn Urd—"

"I can almost guarantee it was not," Haraldr said with an indulgent smile.

I paused in what I had been trying to say. Because as much as I knew he meant well, the simple truth was that his knowledge of the world all came from books. And as impressive and weighty as that knowledge was—and it truly was—I had experienced things he never could.

Both because, as a volva, I could perceive as well as use magic, but also because I had left Villmark. I had gone out into the wilds, not so far as the mountains of Old Norway, but farther than any save possibly Thorbjorn and Loke had ever gone.

And there were things out there that Haraldr preferred to think of as mere tales in a book.

But I knew they were real.

They were real, and—as this rune was struggling to communicate to me—they were things it was going to be my responsibility to keep everyone safe from.

But I didn't want to have that argument now. "Whatever was speaking through Esja told a story like the story of Gullveig from the

Eddas. Gullveig burned three times, and each time returned as a Norn. Even if whatever was inside of Esja was only pretending to be a part of that story, if it still has power over her, surely we already know the means it will use to exert that power again."

"Stories have power," Haraldr agreed. "Particularly with the sorts of entities that love to spin the tales. But you have separated her from the magic inside her house. She hasn't gone back there. Surely after a month with no further signs of this possession, we can rest a little easier?"

"It's only been a month," I said. "I need more than that to relax."

He was smiling at me, and it took me a minute to work out that it was my repeated use of the word "need" that was provoking that response.

"I think I *ought* to sleep on this," I said deliberately, but with a sigh. "Sometimes that helps."

"Of course," he said, and started to get up from the chair again. But I waved him back down, stopping at his chair to help him snug all the layers warmly around him before heading back out into the night.

I thought of the mead hall, with its promise of roasted chicken and vegetables, pastries and cider. But the idea of being in a crowd of people really didn't appeal.

No, what I needed was a quiet night at home. A warmed up can of soup, and an early bedtime with my cat Mjolner tucked up close beside me.

And it was such a pleasant September night for a walk, the air cool but still, with just a hint of smell from the lake out of sight past the ridge to the east. If only I could enjoy it properly.

CHAPTER THREE

THE FIRST PART of my plan worked out great. Mjolner was even waiting for me at the door when I got back to the house. He munched on a bowl of cat food while I heated up a can of tomato soup and even fried up a quick grilled cheese sandwich on my cast-iron skillet to go with it.

Then I took a long, hot bath, soaking under a mountain of soap bubbles, while Mjolner groomed every inch of his sleek black hair meticulously with one six-toed paw.

When the water had gone cold and all the bubbles were gone, I toweled off, pajamaed up, and climbed into bed.

Mjolner waited until I was settled, then curled up against the back of my neck. The soft thrum of his purring never failed to lull me to sleep, but that particular night I didn't even need it. I was asleep before my eyes were half shut, or so it seemed.

But I didn't dream anything useful. No imagery to help me bond with the naudhr rune, no prophetic warnings about Esja and the thing that stalked her.

In my defense, I was only asleep for an hour, maybe two.

Then I was awake, sitting bolt upright in bed with my heart pounding in time to... something.

I wasn't quite sure what had woken me up.

Then the pounding on my front door repeated, and I knew.

I was wearing flannel pajamas, but I still needed to thrust my feet into a pair of slippers before I could comfortably walk across the cold expanses of all my hardwood floors.

And I grabbed the hoodie that was hanging from the back of a chair just by my bedroom door. Because, like the floor, the air had gotten a little chilly since I had gotten out of that tub.

I hustled down the stairs as fast as I could, Mjolner trotting along beside me, then down the nighttime-dark hallway to my front door.

There was no moon out that night, and while the sky was entirely cloudless, the stars felt strangely remote. Like they were dimmer, or further away.

I flung open my door just as a third pounding was starting and saw my friend Nilda Mikkelsen standing there. I knew at once she had just left the ancestral fire. She was wearing the leggings and tooled leather armguards she always wore while performing that martial duty. And her long blonde hair was carefully braided back out of her way, making her look even more like a valkyrie than she usually did.

I mean, even in jeans and a T-shirt, she looked like a valkyrie.

I think it was all the toned muscle in those arms.

But all those impressions flew through my mind like dust escaping a whirlwind, gone faster than they'd even formed.

The impression that lingered was that I had never seen Nilda look as panicked as she did just then.

"What's happened?" I asked, kicking off my slippers to thrust my bare feet into my hiking shoes. Clearly, there wasn't going to be time to change out of my pajamas. But slippers would slow us down, and I could see that speed was going to be of essence.

Mjolner meowed, then bolted back into the shadows of the house behind me. He had his own ways of getting around, faster than mine.

He also had his own priorities in emergencies, and... well, basically, he always had his own priorities. But if I needed him, he would be back at my side before I could even think to call out for him.

So I focused my attention on Nilda. Who was bouncing on her

toes in her impatience for us both to be moving. I made short work of my laces, zipped up my hoodie, and followed her back out into the night.

We reached the village commons and took the turn east towards the lake and towards the caves behind the waterfall that divided Runde from Villmark. Only then did Nilda start talking, although she didn't slow her steps to do so.

"Kara and I were guarding the fire," she said, although that much I had guessed. "Roarr and Esja were down at the mead hall..."

And I threw a quick look back over my shoulder, only then realizing that I didn't actually know they were home. I had just assumed they had made it back while I was sleeping.

I still had no idea what time it was.

But I didn't interrupt as Nilda carried on talking despite the breath-stealing speed of our jogging walk. "...but when the two of them came back up, Esja wanted to sit with Kara and me for a while. We haven't seen her in ages, and we all three wanted to catch up."

We were leaving the edges of the village behind now, slipping past the last of the houses with their neatly fenced-in front gardens, the gates just visible under the glow of the soft LED lights inside their hooded lanterns. Ahead was the stand of birch trees which the path wound snakily through to the meadow beyond.

"Roarr was bored at once, and Esja told him he could go on without her. And we agreed because Valki and Thormund were coming to relieve us at midnight, and Kara and I could walk Esja home once they got there."

Valki was Thorbjorn's father, and Thormund was one of Thorbjorn's four brothers. All five of them are called the Thors, and with their father, they lead all the patrols and guard duties in Villmark.

I had grudgingly gotten Valki to admit that they needed more help, and he had agreed to train other young people to patrol around Villmark. But the ancestral fire he still preferred to assign to only himself, a Thor or a Mikkelsen sister.

That I well knew. But I could hear a desperate urgency in Nilda's voice. And it wasn't hard to work out why.

"That was a sensible plan," I told her, although my words came out in gasps of effort. Nilda could jog for hours without flagging, but I was regretting what I was wearing.

Or rather, what I was not wearing. But it wasn't like I had expected to want a sports bra in the middle of the night when I'd been dressing for bed.

"So Roarr left Esja with you?" I managed to get out between wheezes of breath.

"Yes, he went to see his parents," Nilda said. "I guess he's there still. This was only about half an hour ago."

"Okay, so what happened?" I pressed.

"Esja was talking to us, not about anything in particular. Just chatting, you know? But then she... I guess she was standing closer to the fire than we thought, or something in her clothes just caught..."

I didn't need to hear any more. I dug down deep inside myself and found the will to run, flat-out run, through the last of the birch trees and across the starlit meadow of autumn-dried grasses to the mouth of the cave that lurked in the ground between a few ordinary boulders.

I had to slow my steps a bit down the staircase, as it had formed naturally in the rock over time and was very far from even. But then I reached the cavern below, and I could follow the bright light from the bonfire to the smaller cave that contained our ancestral fire. The flames that had never gone out from the founding of the town so long ago, when my ancestress Torfa had brought her village of people across the world.

The fire that meant safety and protection. How had its flames harmed Esja? It didn't feel like that should even be possible.

But then I burst into the room to see Esja standing on her own two feet. Her clothes were a little singed, and her hair was a tangled mass twisted just at her neck.

I had a moment of absolute relief to see that she was unharmed. That relief spread through my whole body like the warmest honey.

But then Esja turned to me, and I saw only the whites of her eyes. And I realized that, while she was barely speaking loud enough for me to hear, the words she was mumbling under her breath could only be described as raving.

"Thank goodness you're here," Kara said from where she was standing between Esja and the fire. "She's tried to jump into it five times since you left. I'm afraid she's going to get past me and I won't be able to stop her."

"Let's get her out of here," I said, reaching for Esja's shoulders.

She ducked and shimmied out of my grasp, taking three stumbling steps back until Kara caught her then pushed her away from the fire.

And the whole time, Esja's mouth never stopped muttering those words.

"What's she saying?" I asked.

"I can't catch a word of it," Kara said.

"I think she's speaking in an older dialect," Nilda told me. "Some of the words I *can* catch, they sound like my great-grandmother's accent. From what I can remember of it from when I was little, anyway."

"We have to get her out of this room," Kara said, blowing a strand of hair that had escaped from her braid out of her sweaty face. I could only imagine how hot she was, standing as close to the fire as she was. That bonfire burned with a blistering intensity. I was uncomfortable in my cotton pajamas, and I was across the room from it.

"Ingrid?" Nilda said.

"Right," I said, and reached for Esja again.

This time, my hands caught her narrow shoulders.

And at that touch, she just stopped moving. She stopped babbling. She stopped trying to get into the fire.

She stopped trying to evade me and just slumped against me.

Nilda and Kara both raced forward, as if afraid that I was about to crumple under the slight weight of Esja.

Although I did notice that Esja was less slight than she had been even the month before when she'd moved into my house. Her former sickly frame was very much a thing of the past, although it was my persistent mental image of her.

But I really needed to correct that mental image. Because even slumped in a faint against me, Esja was starting to look nearly as valkyrie-like as either of the Mikkelsen sisters.

Esja sucked in a deep breath, then looked up at me. Her eyes were clear and blue, just as they should be. They were also filled with confusion.

"Do you know where you are?" I asked her.

"The cave behind the waterfall," she said at once.

"Do you remember what happened?" I asked.

That brought a frown to her face. "I ate dinner. I had about half a dozen cinnamon buns, but only half a tankard of mulled cider. It's so strong. I made Roarr finish mine as well as his."

Then she blinked and looked around the cave, as if just then realizing that Roarr wasn't there.

"Then what happened?" I pressed her.

Her frown deepened. "I danced with Roarr a couple of times. Then I danced with Michelle and Jessica to some fast songs. But Roarr said it was getting late, and he was worried because you'd never come down even though you'd kind of said you didn't think you *were* coming down."

She shot me a look that was just short of being accusatory, but I said nothing.

Then she looked around at the cave with its racks of weapons, the heavy stone that stood ready to block passage to the waterfall and Runde beyond, and the bonfire that dominated the center of the room.

"I don't remember coming here," she admitted at last. "Where's Roarr?"

"Roarr is safe," I told her. "He went to see his parents. You stayed here to talk to Nilda and Kara. Does that sound familiar at all to you?"

She pondered it with a furrowed brow, but in the end, just shook her head. "No. Sorry. I remember dancing, and then I remember looking up at you. Nothing in between."

Then her eyes went round and wide and she whispered to me, "Did I do something again? Something bad? Like before?"

"No," I assured her. "No, you just singed your clothes a little and were upset. That's why Nilda came to get me. You must've had a shock, although Kara and Nilda put out the fire on your clothes before you were burned. Let's get home, get you cleaned up, and get to bed. We'll see how things look in the morning. All right?"

Esja nodded mutely, and after a silent farewell to the Mikkelsens, I guided her out of the cave and back up into the starlight.

Roarr and I had, by mutual agreement, not told Esja a lot about the things she had done the last time she had been out of her head. But it wasn't entirely surprising that she had concluded it had been bad.

It had, indeed, been bad. It might have been catastrophic, if Roarr and I hadn't been there to stop it.

She had been summoning raw chaos. And the fact that I still didn't know for what purpose she had been used to do that made the whole situation all the more chilling.

Keeping her from leaving Villmark for the wilds to the north was the obvious first step. And easily enough done. All the patrols on the roads had already been ordered not to let her out of town without me.

But now I was caught in a real conundrum. Did I hope that she remembered anything in the morning? Or was it better if she forgot?

Even if forgetting meant none of us would ever know just what she had been muttering under her breath? While effectively dancing around our ancestral fire?

The flames that were known to spark visions of power?

That fire had brought out Kara's innate magic. It was entirely possible it could do the same with Esja.

But Esja was far from Kara's solid, stable personality. And she was already struggling so much with my grandmother's teachings on protective magic.

If she unlocked more power inside herself, the danger it would simply consume her was so very, very high.

And, most maddening for me, I was in yet another situation where all I could usefully do was practice patience.

I was so sick of practicing patience.

CHAPTER FOUR

ESJA and I were just entering the village commons from the east when I saw Mjolner approaching from the west, with Roarr close at his heels.

Roarr was following the cat, but he looked distinctly confused when Mjolner didn't turn toward my townhouse. Still, he kept on past the brick walls of the common well until he finally saw the two of us coming towards him. Then the confusion on his face melted into a look of relief that he hadn't been crazy to follow my cat.

But that relief was short-lived. As soon as he saw that I was walking with an arm around Esja, guiding her over the cobble-stoned road, he seemed to put all the pieces together without me having to explain a thing. He rushed over and grabbed Esja by both of her arms. She looked up at him, startled, but he just gazed fixedly into her blue eyes.

"I don't see anything," he said at last. "Maybe I should look again when we get inside, though."

"I feel fine," Esja said. But not with any real conviction.

"I'm glad Mjolner found you," I said to Roarr. "Esja nearly set herself on fire in the cave behind the waterfall. Kara and Nilda put her out before she got really hurt, but she was raving afterward for quite some time. Not that I could catch any of the words."

"I remember nothing of this," Esja told him.

"Oh," Roarr said. "I wished I had gotten there sooner. When she was still... you know."

"Me too," I said, but just indicated we should all keep walking.

We got back to my house and turned on all the lights, but even with a second, more thorough look, Roarr didn't see any sign of what he called the un-thing lingering around Esja.

I looked too, with all of my magical perceptions. I even tried drawing her portrait, just a quick and dirty charcoal sketch, but saw nothing there either. Not that I expected much. When Esja was having troubles before, Roarr had noticed more than I had. I doubted that situation had changed in the last month.

He didn't know what he was sensing, but I had come to rely on the fact that he sensed *something* even when I didn't.

"You should get some sleep," I told Esja.

"I do feel weirdly tired," she said. "I mean, I know it's pretty late. But it's more tired than that."

"Something magical did happen to you, and as much as you didn't make it happen, just channeling it through you can be exhausting," I said. "Get some sleep. Hopefully, you'll remember more in the morning. But if not, we can go back down to Runde and see what my mormor thinks."

Esja pursed her lips—she was never wildly enthusiastic about seeing my grandmother—but just nodded and headed up the stairs.

"I'm going to make some coffee," Roarr said. "I'll set a chair in the hallway and keep watch outside her bedroom door. Just in case."

I didn't think that was entirely necessary, but I could tell from the set of his jaw that there was no point in trying to talk him out of it. Staying with us in order to watch over Esja was not a job he had wanted to choose for himself, but he took it seriously all the same.

"I'll be in my room if you need me," I said.

I climbed back into my bed, shivering until the covers finally warmed up again enough for me to drift back to sleep. Mjolner purred softly against the back of my neck, and I think I was dreaming of being out on a boat on the lake. His purr was dream-morphed into the soft suss-suss of water against the hull of the boat.

I could even feel the warmth of the sun on my face and the cold spray of water from the lake in perfect counterpoint.

But then I was sitting upright with my heart racing fast once more. Someone was pounding on my door again. Only now I had heard it the first time.

I thrust my feet back into their slippers and pulled on my hoodie. I nearly collided with Roarr outside my bedroom door, apparently about to come get me.

"It's Thormund," he told me. "I let him in. He's in the kitchen. I told him to help himself to the coffee. I made plenty."

"Thanks, Roarr," I said.

Thormund was supposed to be on duty at the ancestral fire with Valki. The two of them were meant to relieve the Mikkelsens at midnight, or so Nilda had said. So something *else* had happened at the fire?

Maybe it would be a good idea for me to take some of those shifts myself. Just to see what was happening.

Thormund's large frame dominated my little kitchen space as he stood over my sink, carefully pouring coffee from the carafe of my coffeemaker into the largest of my mugs. The one his brother usually used when he was in my house.

Thormund was the one of Thorbjorn's four brothers that I actually knew the least well.

Thorge, the second youngest, I had spent the most time with since even before he had married Kara Mikkelsen.

Thorulv, the oldest, had come to me for help a couple of months ago when Thoralv, the youngest, had gotten himself into quite a bit of trouble. They had stumbled between camps of different alv tribes and had nearly gotten mixed up in a war between them. But Thorbjorn and I had managed to get Thoralv out safely, to Thorulv's eternal relief.

But Thormund? I couldn't recall actually ever exchanging more than the merest of pleasantries with him.

He was the second oldest. He generally fought with a spear roughly the size of a Scottish caber. And he wore his long reddish-blond hair in three thick braids that fell halfway down his back, and his beard was divided into two equally long braids. But most of that I only knew because, as an artist, I had drawn him as well as his brothers many times.

Who he was as a person, I had never gotten to know.

Well, no time like the present.

"Thormund," I said as I came into the kitchen.

Thormund turned with a hand extended towards me, and I realized that while standing over my sink he had filled two mugs with coffee. I took the mug he was offering me with the smallest of sighs.

Clearly, sleep was not happening this night.

I went to the icebox to fetch my little pitcher of cream, but Thormund was already sipping at his, still black. And, knowing Roarr, made extra strong and bitter. But he just made a grunt of appreciation and gave the mug a little satisfied nod.

"Is it the fire again?" I asked as I poured a measure of cream into my mug and stirred it in with a spoon.

"The fire?" he said, but then seemed to put together what I was saying. "No. Nilda and Kara told me about that, but no. This is something else. Maybe nothing that involves you at all, but my father wanted you to know what was going on."

"Now, in the middle of the night," I said as I took a sip of my coffee. The warmth, at least, was welcome. "It must be serious."

"It's definitely serious," Thormund said. "I'm just not sure it involves you."

"Tell us," Roarr said from the doorway. He was standing in the hall, far enough back to still keep an eye on the stairway in case Esja should try to sneak down, but close enough to hear the conversation inside the kitchen.

"Three women have gone missing," Thormund said, setting his coffee aside as if the topic and the beverage absolutely did not go together in his mind. He crossed his arms and scowled down at my tiled floor. "One last night, one the night before, and a third this very night."

"And this is the first I'm hearing of it?" I asked, shocked.

"It wasn't immediately clear that anything was wrong at first," he said. "Two nights ago, Vigdis Olafsdottir was out with friends at Ullr's hall but never made it home."

I was about to demand again why no one had told me, but Roarr made a little sound of recognition in his throat. I spun to pin him with a gaze demanding an explanation.

"Sorry, I don't know if you know Vigdis at all," Roarr said. "She's a bit... wild. I'm sure if no one knew where she was for two days, they'd just assume she'd holed up with some new paramour, or was sleeping off a truly epic night."

"For two days?" I still had to demand.

Roarr just shrugged.

"We knew about her yesterday," Thormund put in. "Her parents came to see my father. They were... somewhat concerned, but not alarmed. It was like her to not come home after a night out, but they were still worried. My father promised the patrols would watch out for her and let them know if she was seen around town. This was before the second woman disappeared."

"And who was she?" I asked.

"Dalla Leifsdottir," Thormund said.

Roarr made a sort of choking sound, but this time I ignored him, keeping my eyes on Thormund.

"Who is she? Another wild girl?" I asked. Perhaps a bit too aggressively.

"No," Thormund said. "Dalla is eighty-four."

"Eighty-four?" I repeated.

"And she was taken at night?" Roarr asked.

"We don't know if anyone was taken," Thormund said. "We just know they've disappeared. Vigdis was last seen parting ways from her friends outside Ullr's hall. Dalla was last seen leaving as the marketplace was closing down last night. Or, I guess, the night before? It's morning now, isn't it?"

"She was out shopping and never made it home?" I asked.

"Yes. She lives with her granddaughter's family. She was running out for a handful of fresh dill for something her granddaughter was preparing for dinner. It was meant to be just a short trip, but she never made it back," Thormund said.

"And that's when you started to get more than medium concerned about Vigdis?" I asked.

"Honestly, they didn't seem related at first," Thormund said. "Only in the sense that we told all the patrols to watch for either of the two of them. But no one has seen any sign of either."

"And now there's a third," I said, taking another sip of my coffee. I was going to need the caffeine, and soon.

"Geira Palnisdottir," Thormund said. "She had just sent her two young children into the house for dinner and was picking up their toys from the garden. The toys were left in a pile outside her door, but there was no sign of her at all."

"No sign of a struggle. No one heard a scream. Nothing?" I said.

"Nothing," Thormund agreed. "And with the requests to watch out for the first two women, the patrols have been extra alert. But no one reported anything."

"That's why Valki wanted you," Roarr guessed.

"I wished I had known about this sooner," I said.

"Patrolling the streets is our duty, not yours," Thormund said. Then he finished off the rest of his mug of coffee in one long swallow. "However, now it is clear we need your help. My father is still at the fire, and the patrols are still walking the streets. But I am at your disposal. What would you like to do?"

"I need to get dressed and grab my art bag," I said. "Then I'll need to see the last places each of these women were seen. And hopefully we'll have a lead to go on from there."

"I'll stay here with Esja?" Roarr guessed.

"Please," I said.

As horrifying as this situation was already becoming in my own mind, I had at least that little bit of comfort.

Knowing Esja was safe at home, I could focus on other things.

But I had to admit that sense of comfort kicked up a notch as I saw Roarr move his chair to Esja's doorway before silently easing that door open a few inches. We could both see her there, sleeping peacefully in her bed.

I just hoped that remained true. And that the fates of the three missing women weren't as dark as I feared.

CHAPTER FIVE

THORMUND WAS as stalwart as any of his brothers, following by my side as I moved from location to location in Villmark, assisting when it was obvious something was needed but otherwise standing back and out of the way.

Alas, dawn found us still out in the streets, knowing nothing more than we'd known before I'd started.

None of my drawings told me anything. And, as the patrols had reported, there was zero evidence anywhere of any struggle. Not so much as a broken branch or a scrap of clothing. No one had heard a noise.

It was like three women on three different nights had just... walked away. Without a word to anyone.

But I was sure that wasn't true. None of the patrols had seen any of them. And they watched every path out of town very closely. They would've seen anyone who tried to leave.

The image my tired mind kept conjuring was aliens pulling them up into the sky in a cone of light. But that didn't feel likely. I'd just watched way more TV than the average Villmarker.

I certainly didn't mention this theory to Thormund.

In the end, exhausted, I just brought him with me to speak to his father at the ancestral fire.

"All the women were taken after dark?" I asked. Not for the first time.

"That is correct," Valki said.

"Then let's double the patrols at sunset tonight," I said. "And I'll go out with them. Maybe we can catch this before it happens again."

Although I had no idea how I hoped to do that.

"It will be done," Valki said, putting a fist over his heart in a very formal sort of gesture.

"I'll patrol by your side," Thormund vowed.

"I appreciate that," I said.

Then I headed back home for some much needed and much delayed sleep. It was the sort of fitful daytime sleeping that never did me much good. I woke up hours later, still exhausted, and still with no idea what was happening in my town.

And, obviously, with no better sense of my relationship to the naudhr rune.

I forced myself to eat some kind of dinner, then filled up on an inadvisable amount of coffee. I was just checking the contents of my art bag when I heard footsteps coming down the stairs.

I looked up, and for a moment, I was confused. I wasn't looking at either of the Mikkelsens, I knew, but it was like they had a long lost third sister I had never met.

Then I realized I was looking at Esja. She was dressed just as the Mikkelsens liked to dress, in leggings and a loose-fitting tunic belted at the waist with a wide leather belt. She had tooled leather armguards strapped to her forearms, and there was a sword and a pair of knives on her belt.

"What's this?" I said, equal parts amused and alarmed.

"I'm going out on patrol," Esja announced, tossing back a long braid of fair blonde hair.

"Are you?" I said, amusement fading fast.

"The patrols have been doubled," she told me, as if this were news to me. But then again, she had no idea why I had been sleeping all day.

"Everyone is short-handed. Kara and Nilda said I could patrol with them if I brought Roarr with me, and Roarr agreed."

I frowned at that, and peered further up into the shadows at the top of the stairs.

"I said I agreed if you agreed," Roarr hurried to say. "And only because I haven't seen a single sign of a problem around her all day."

"I'm fine," Esja said.

"She's not wrong about the short-handedness," Roarr added. "Everyone is needed, at least for tonight. Hopefully, this gets resolved soon."

I said nothing. But my scowl probably said enough.

"Ingrid, I'll never leave her side. Not even for an instant," he said.

"And neither will Nilda and Kara," Esja put in. "And I won't wander off, I swear."

I chewed at my lip. But after my night of sketching all around Villmark, I had learned at least one thing.

There was a pattern to the disappearances. Vigdis had last been seen at Ullr's hall, which was on the far end of Villmark from where she lived.

Dalla had been on her way home from the marketplace, which was only a short two blocks from her granddaughter's home.

And Geira had been in her own front garden, mere steps from the doorway into her home.

The range was getting shorter, a lot shorter, between each victim and her closest safe haven with each disappearance.

It was entirely possible the next victim would be taken from their own home.

As much as I hated to admit it, Esja was probably safer out in the streets with the Mikkelsens and Roarr both watching over her than she would be at home with just Roarr.

Especially a Roarr that I could tell was champing at the bit to contribute more than babysitting. He wanted to be out with the patrols as badly as Esja did.

"I don't like the fact that I missed taking you to see my mormor today," I said with a sigh. "But that couldn't be helped. I have everyone's vow of good behavior. I guess I'll just have to content myself with that."

"I swear I'll be good," Esja said, all in a rush.

I just nodded. "Come on," I said. "We should get to the commons and meet the others."

There was a thick crowd of people milling about the commons all around the well. It seemed I wasn't the only one thinking that being in the street in groups was better than being home alone.

Although Valki was already taking command, sending everyone with young children down the hill to the council meeting hall. They could be safe in a group behind those heavy doors. No one was going to be out patrolling with a child in their party.

I also noticed that Thormund wasn't the only Thor currently in Villmark when I saw another head of bright red hair towering over the men crowded around him. He wasn't quite facing my way, but there was no mistaking which Thor it was. Not with the sides shaved to show off the knot work tattoos that arched over both of his ears. It had to be Thorge.

He was currently speaking with Raggi and Skefill, and I decided the last thing my evening needed was time spent with either of those two. They were isolationists, and I was still an outsider in their eyes despite my earned and widely respected station as their volva. We had butted heads on many occasions.

Sure, they were in the village commons now because they were part of the regular patrols, always helping out to protect the people of Villmark.

But that didn't make either of their personalities any easier for me to get along with.

"Ingrid, Nilda and Kara are just over there?" Esja said, tugging at my elbow.

"Go ahead," I told her. "Stay safe," I added, mostly to Roarr.

He gave me a little bow. Then the two of them jogged over to where the Mikkelsens were standing just beyond Thorge.

"Ready?" Thormund asked, suddenly at my elbow.

"Are we joining up with any of the active patrols?" I asked.

"We can if you like, but I thought for what you do, moving apart from the others might make more sense," he said.

"Maybe so," I said. "But let's not stray too far from the others."

"Of course," he said. "We'll stop when you wish to draw, but otherwise let's trail closely behind the Mikkelsens party?"

"Perfect," I said.

The groups were just starting to break up and move away from the village commons as the last of the sun's rays sank down behind the tree-topped hills to the west. The majority of the people who had gathered in the square headed south now, following Valki to the council hall. I watched young families with children in tow, or even still in arms, huddling close together in whispering knots as they drifted past.

And it was still perfectly lovely weather. That felt so ironic to me. But quite aside from our grim mission, it was a gorgeous fall night for a walk. The air was still warm from the fading day, but an ever so slightly chill breeze was blowing in from over the lake. It carried the smell of lake water but also of the many pine trees it must have wended its way through to reach us in the center of Villmark. Sharp and refreshing.

The Mikkelsens were heading south, albeit on a road that was a few blocks east of the main road the families were using to get to the council hall. Thormund and I trailed behind, just far enough back that the sounds of their voices were a mere murmur at the edge of my awareness.

Even Thormund close at my side didn't intrude much on my awareness as we walked. It was like he was making himself unobtrusive, his footfalls almost silent on the cobblestones, and his breathing slow and controlled.

All of that made it so easy for me to slide into a semi-fugue state, one where I could perceive magic as easily as I saw the sun by day.

I could see a brightness off to the east, the glow from my mormor's mead hall with all of its elaborate spells protecting it.

There was a soft sense of magic coming from the direction of my own house in town. But I knew that sense well. It was Mjolner, napping on my pillow.

But nothing else was making itself felt to me at all.

And as we fell even further behind the Mikkelsens' party, all of that quiet started to get to me.

"Thorbjorn has been gone for quite some time," I said at last, just to break the silence. "Is your mom doing okay with that?"

"She's used to it," Thormund said with a shrug. Then he shot me a sidelong look with a gleam to his eye. "We were all gone longer than he's been now, back before you and the Mikkelsens fetched us from that tower where we were being held captive."

"I'm hoping I don't have to do that again," I said.

"I'm sure Thorbjorn is fine," Thormund said. "I guess I was just trying to say thanks. For before."

"No thanks needed," I said. "But you're quite welcome."

We walked a little further in companionable silence. Thormund started to speak again, but whatever he had been intending to say was abandoned as we both stopped cold in the middle of the street.

Or, rather, the cold stopped us. It was like a ghost or something had just passed through our bodies, gone as soon as it was there. I touched the ends of my hair, half expecting to feel ice forming there.

Thormund beside me shivered despite the heavy cloak he was wearing around his shoulders.

"You felt it too?" I whispered to him.

"An icy wind, but not a wind?" he asked. I nodded. "Yes. I felt it too. It passed from south to north. Which winds tend not to do."

"It also didn't stir up any air, which wind definitely doesn't tend to do," I said.

We were both still whispering. Like we didn't want to do anything that might invite that ghostly freezing feeling to return.

"Shall we see where it goes?" Thormund said, although with the air of someone who was desperately hoping the answer would be no.

"Where it goes, or where it came from?" I pondered.

Then we heard something that hadn't been heard at all the last three nights.

We heard a scream rending the night.

The scream had come from the south. With only an exchange of glances between us, we both at once started running that way.

Toward the source of whatever had just passed through us? Maybe.

But definitely towards the last place we had seen the Mikkelsen patrol. I hadn't realized we had lost sight of them, but we had.

And, running now, they weren't coming into sight.

I swallowed down panic and just kept running. Running as if my life depended on it.

Or someone's life, anyway.

CHAPTER SIX

THE NORTH-SOUTH ROADS in Villmark ran up and down the hillside, so they always had some degree of slope. Where Thormund and I had been when we'd heard the scream was just a block off the market street, which was situated on a long, almost level east-west ridge on the hillside.

But now we were running south of that ridge, and the road here was steep enough to be treacherous in the moonless starlight. Worse, we were on a road little bigger than an alley, and the only streetlights were on the corners with the large crossroads. And—given that all the lights in Villmark were shuttered to shine only straight down, and were low output LED lights at that—it was nearly too dark to see as we ran.

Basically, we were in a place about as dark as it got inside the confines of Villmark. The walls that enclosed the front gardens around us rose to a level just above the top of my head. Thormund could maybe see over them into the gardens beyond and the lights gently illuminating the front doors, but I could not.

Luckily, we didn't have far to go before we could hear the sounds of voices ahead of us. There was a crossroads there, I knew, an east-west road lined with residences meeting the north-south road we were following, also lined with residences.

There were a lot of voices, all talking at once in a confusion of noise. But I could make out Nilda's voice speaking calmly to a woman who was nearly hysterical in her sobbing.

Then I saw Kara standing in the middle of the road looking uphill to where she could no doubt hear Thormund and I approaching, he in his heavy boots and me in my hiking shoes that were slapping loudly as I ran.

"There's a girl—" Kara started to say, when the hysterical woman let out another shriek. Only this time it was a shriek of relief tinged with frustration. But I also sensed the promise of anger to come once the relief had had a moment to sink in to her mind.

"Disa!" the woman said. Thormund and I had skidded to a halt beside Kara, but from there we were close enough to see the woman with Nilda's hand on her arm. Her face was flushed and tear-stained, but her eyes were on a row of low shrubs growing just outside the open gate of a front garden to one of the houses.

The shrubs had been rustling, but they stopped now. Strangely, that sudden stillness to the autumn-dry twigs and leaves had an air of hesitancy to it.

"Disa?" Nilda said, also to the shrubs.

"I'm here, Mor!" a little girl's voice answered. Then she appeared, her braids pulled loose and long strands of her hair catching on every single branch on her way out. She was five, maybe six, and extremely dirty.

"Disa! Don't you *ever* do that again!" the woman chastised, even as she caught the girl up in the fiercest of mama bear hugs.

"All's well?" Thormund asked as his eyes scanned our surroundings for any signs of danger the others might have missed. Clearly another patrol had reached this source of the scream before Thormund and I had, as four men with the build of farmers were standing around Nilda. A few looked familiar from my time visiting all the farms south of Villmark the month before, but none of their names were coming to mind in that moment.

"Yes. It seems Disa here was just playing a little trick on her mother," Nilda said.

"So, no one is missing?" I asked. I could hear more voices and footsteps closing in on us from all four directions. The other nearby patrols, drawn by the sound of Disa's mother's scream.

"Well—" Kara started to say.

"I'm here," Esja said as she stepped up behind me. "I was just looking into those shadows over there. There's nothing there, though."

"You were supposed to stay close," Kara reminded her.

"I wasn't far," Esja insisted. "I stayed in the light."

"Who was taken?" someone in one of the other patrols asked. I squinted in the dim light and just made out the close-cut, thinning blond hair of Raggi as he stood with his hood thrown back, glaring at Nilda and then at me.

"No one," I said. "False alarm."

He scowled, as if the false alarm had somehow been my doing.

"We need to break up this crowd," I said, but more loudly so everyone at the crossroads could hear me. "Everyone, get back on your patrol routes. We can't let this misunderstanding distract us."

Most of the others snapped to at once, nodding their acceptance of my orders before heading back up the roads they had come down.

But Raggi was still standing there with that scowl on his face.

"Is there something I can help you with, Raggi?" I asked him.

"Where's Roarr?" he asked. "Isn't he supposed to be with the Mikkelsens? I find it a tad suspicious that he doesn't seem to be with them now."

I looked around and realized, to my annoyance, that he was right. There was no sign of Roarr anywhere.

I turned to Esja, but she just shrugged. "He was standing right next to me before I went to look at those shadows. I thought he was right here."

"You both promised me that you would stay together. What did you see in those shadows that distracted you so greatly?" I asked her.

But she just shrugged again. "I guess it was a kind of feeling? But it was nothing. There was nothing lurking in the shadows. I was just imagining things."

"We're all a little jumpy," Kara put in.

"We're jumpy for a reason," Raggi snarled at her. "Three women are missing."

"I didn't say there wasn't a reason," Kara snapped back. "I'm just saying, jumping at shadows is something that's going to happen. But we need to stay sane here."

Thorge stepped up beside her without saying a word, but his mere presence seemed to calm her. She let her hackles down again with a nod to Raggi, then shot a glance at Esja as if double-checking that she was still there with us all.

"Esja had a feeling she should check out those shadows," Kara went on, more calmly now. "And she did. She checked them out. She confirmed there was no cause for alarm. So she moved on."

"And the scream was just a momentary panic," Nilda said. "A childhood prank. But not one Disa is going to repeat."

She shot the girl in question a dour look, and the dirty little girl cowered behind her mother's skirts but still managed a solemn nod, promising not to do it again.

"We need to get back out on patrol," I said. "Standing around here is not keeping anyone safe."

"I'm not going anywhere until I see Roarr Egilsen," Raggi said.

Skefill stepped up beside him and crossed his arms, a silent ditto.

I sighed and rubbed at my head. I hated dealing with these two. And I didn't hate it any less when I kind of thought they were right.

But before I had to come up with a response, someone else rescued the moment.

"Roarr is here," Thormund said as he emerged from a dark alley that ran between two fenced gardens. It was filled with more of the scrubby bushes like Disa had been hiding in, and judging from the random bits of broken toys and dropped candy that lurked beneath those bushes, was largely used by the neighborhood kids as a shortcut or hiding place.

Roarr was standing behind Thormund with his hands in his pockets, looking a little chagrined.

"Where were you?" I asked him levelly. But I could sense Raggi just out of the periphery of my vision, leaning forward to catch whatever Roarr said in response.

"I was looking for Esja," he said. "Nilda and Kara were helping that woman calm down and look for her child, but Esja wasn't there. I thought she might have gone down this alley..." He ended with a chagrined shrug.

"I was just down there," Esja said, pointing one house over from where Disa had been hiding.

"I'm not sure how I missed seeing you," he said.

"Did you think you saw something moving in that alley?" I asked him.

He shook his head a little noncommittally.

"Did you find anything in there while you were looking for Esja?" I asked him.

He shook his head again, more definitively this time.

"That's where the man was," Disa suddenly said, then ducked back out of sight behind her mother again.

"What man?" Nilda asked her.

"There was a man in the alley," Disa said, her little voice gaining confidence.

"This man?" I asked her, pointing at Roarr.

She squinted at him, squeezing shut first one eye and then the other.

It felt to me like she was soaking up all the attention, shooting little glances at Raggi and Skefill as they glowered at Roarr. Then, when she thought she had their tempers at maximum simmer, she suddenly opened both eyes and said, "Yes. Just like him. A dark, scary man."

Thormund made a strangled sort of sound that took me a minute to recognize as choked back laughter. So he was no more convinced by Disa's little show than I was.

With a side of not seeing Roarr as either dark or scary, perhaps.

But Raggi and Skefill both had moved their hands to the hilts of their weapons.

"Disa and her mother need to get to the council hall with the other families," Thorge said.

"We were heading that way, but Disa forgot something at home and we went back for it," Disa's mother said.

Disa pulled a hand out from behind her back and showed us all a little painted wooden horse with what appeared to be real horsehair forming its mane and the long swoop of its tail. A well-loved toy.

But certainly not worth risking being abducted for.

"Raggi, Skefill, please escort them both to the hall, then resume your patrol," Thormund said in a booming voice not even the two of them were going to argue with.

Although I could sense how badly they both wanted to.

"What about him?" Raggi asked, jutting his chin towards Roarr.

"Roarr is going to patrol with me," Thorge said. "If he ducks into another dark alley, I'll be ducking in after him."

Raggi and Skefill exchanged a long look. Skefill gave in first with a careless shrug. Raggi scowled again, but put a politer look on his face before gesturing for Disa's mother to accompany them west to the better lit main road towards the council hall.

"We'll watch Esja," Kara told me. Then scoffed out a self-directed laugh before adding, "We'll watch her more closely."

"*You* watch her," I said. "It's pretty clear this all went down the way it did because everyone thought someone else was watching what, in fact, *no one* was watching. Nilda focuses on the patrol sweep. You focus on Esja."

"And Esja focuses on staying with the group," Esja said.

She was standing too far back into the shadows for me to say for sure, but I thought I sensed an eye roll accompanying those words.

"Roarr?" I said.

He looked at Esja, then shook his head at me.

"What's this?" Thorge asked.

"Nothing. I'm ready," Roarr said.

He and Thorge headed off to the east, and the Mikkelsens with Esja continued their southward patrolling.

Thormund was looking at me intently, though. So rather than follow closely behind them, I let them go on ahead for a moment so I could look up at him.

The twinkle in his green eyes was so reminiscent of his brother Thorbjorn's that I felt like my heart was up in my throat, choking me, but I managed a single word. "What?"

"You're uniquely worried about that one," he said.

"I am," I admitted.

"Because her brother Loke Grímsson is your friend?" he asked.

"Partly," I said.

But he wasn't fooled by my attempt to distract him with a non-answer. He just looked down at me, those green eyes still teasing me.

"Something is going on with Esja," I admitted with a sigh. "Something my mormor and I already know about. There are protections around Esja now, and I'm having the others keep an eye on her, just as an extra precaution. I'm probably being paranoid, being so worried. On the other hand, I should probably have sent her down to my mormor rather than letting her patrol."

He accepted this answer with a more solemn nod. But then he said, "That might have been wise. But my own thought is that she just would've slipped away from you if you'd tried."

"Because she's trouble?" I asked. I had really hoped her wild girl days were behind her. The last month had been so peaceful.

But, it turned out, that wasn't what Thormund had meant at all.

"She has valkyrie in her," he said. "Just look at her with the Mikkelsens. They all glow like direct descendants of those shining shield maidens from the past."

I could still see them, walking together in the patch of another streetlight much further down the road.

And at that distance, Thormund was right. I couldn't tell one from the other at all. They were all total valkyries.

Whatever danger was stalking the streets of Villmark, I didn't think it stood much of a chance taking any of those three.

"Come on," I said anyway. "Let's catch up before they get too far ahead of us."

"Let's," he agreed.

My feet were already aching from the walk, but I knew without looking at my watch that the night was not even half over.

It was, in fact, far, far from over.

CHAPTER SEVEN

THORMUND and I spent hours together, walking all the way to the south end of the town, then turning to take the next block over back to the north end of town.

We saw nothing. The only thing to be heard was occasionally the distant sound of another patrol walking together and speaking in soft voices to each other.

The Mikkelsens and Esja were visible to us every time they passed under a streetlight. Nothing about the three of them ever seemed amiss.

We had turned at the far north end of town to head south once more, yet another block further to the east, and I was finding it harder and harder to stay awake.

Then we passed the marketplace, all shuttered darkness at this hour, and then the east-west road that Disa and her mother lived on.

And Thormund softly cleared his throat before saying, "What was that thing we felt before?"

"I was wondering the same thing," I said. "I thought at first it had something to do with someone being abducted, only since no one was taken, I'm not sure."

"Maybe something was thwarted in an attempt?" Thormund said.

"Maybe," I said, but I wasn't sure.

"We can keep a close eye on Esja and the Mikkelsens if you like," he said.

But it was pretty clear that he was voicing half of a two-option proposition.

And anyway, the weight of the art bag on my shoulder had been digging into my flesh for some time now.

"No," I gave in with a sigh. "Let's go back to where we felt that cold pass through us. I'd like to try drawing there."

Although what good it could do, I had no idea. It was so dark there. Waiting for daylight had a strong appeal.

Only I was still holding out a hope that at dawn, I'd be able to collapse into my bed and sleep most of the sunlit hours away.

Thormund, whose memory seemed better than mine, led the way through a mini-labyrinth of alleys to the exact spot we'd been standing when we'd felt that cold and heard that scream.

There was nothing remarkable about it now. The cobblestones were gleaming ever so softly in the starlight as they accumulated a light coating of dew in preparation for the coming day. But other than that, the air was as unseasonably warm as it had been every night that month.

And the few breezes that passed through were lake-chill, carrying with them the scents of the coast off to our east. But that was a far cry from the bone-chilling cold we had both felt hours before.

One of the nearby houses had a small stone bench standing outside the gate to their front garden. I brushed the dew away with the sleeve of my hoodie, then sat down, letting my bag drop to the ground with a groan of relief. Then I dug inside of it, finding my sketchbook and a couple of graphite pencils.

Good enough for drawing in total darkness. The nearest street-light was still too far away to illuminate the page before me. But the starlight had it glowing just a touch. Enough for me to see the pencil marks on the paper if I made them reasonably dark.

"Should I stay close or move away?" Thormund asked.

Which was a good question. I pondered it. How much was his

energy like Thorbjorn? Enough to soothe my magical mind? Or enough to be a distraction?

"Stand behind me," I decided at last. "Close enough to watch over me in case I attract something, but not in my field of view." Then I scoffed out a little laugh. "It's not like you're going to block my light or anything."

Thormund nodded, then settled himself just behind me. It was actually a tight squeeze, as the bench was off the side of the road, very close to the fence for the house's front garden. But he leaned back against that fence, hands resting on the shaft of the spear that he kept planted between the toes of his boots, rather like a hiker taking a break with their hiking stick at the ready.

I chewed at my lip for a moment, but the minute my pencil tip touched the paper, my magical artistic side took over. The graphite filled the paper almost without needing any input from me. My hand was just a guide to get the drawing on the page, or else it would just flow out of me to hang invisibly in the air.

I always lost track of time and awareness of my surroundings when I drew like this. I called it my fugue state. It put my deeper mind in touch with things my surface mind couldn't perceive.

But there wasn't always anything there to *be* perceived. I couldn't find clues that weren't there to be found, after all.

I knew something had happened here. And Thormund had felt it too.

Still, when I came back out of my fugue state to find I had drawn page after page of nothing but views of Lake Superior, I couldn't help feeling a spasm of disappointment.

"The breezes smell of the lake," Thormund said, sensing from the change in my movements that the need for silence had passed. "But that cold I felt, it wasn't a breeze."

"No, I agree," I said.

"It wasn't the chill from a breeze, but perhaps it was still a chill from the lake?" he pondered.

"I don't know," I admitted. "Perhaps it's just reminding me of the lake. Like, as a symbol. I don't know what's happening here, and it's upsetting me. But just being out on that lake on the longship is upsetting to me, too."

"You don't like our longship?" he asked.

"I love our longship," I assured him. "It's the lake that freaks me out. The icy depths, you know?"

He leaned over his spear, peering down at the page open on my lap. It was a particularly dense drawing of the lake, the heart of it so filled with dark strokes of graphite that its surface was shiny in that way that heavy, layered pencil marks could do.

"Maybe," he said, even more ponderously than before.

But then I sensed a change in the sounds around us. The patrol sounds were louder, and more localized to the area north of us.

To the village commons.

"Something is happening," Thormund said. But I was already stowing my sketchbook and pencils.

We jogged back up the lane until we reached the better lit environs of the village commons.

Most of the other patrols were gathering there, talking together in urgent little groups. But dawn was still hours away, I was sure of it. And the only people who would call back all the patrols were Thormund and me.

Or Valki, if he had left the council hall.

"Thorge," Thormund said, pointing his brother out to me.

The two of us jogged to where Thorge was speaking with another patrol of all men. These men had their hoods up and their faces were lost to the shadows.

"Thorge," Thormund said as we approached.

"Thormund. Ingrid," Thorge said. But I didn't like the tense look to his face.

"What's happened?" I asked.

"Someone is missing," he said.

I immediately looked around for Esja, but almost as immediately found her. She was standing closer to the well, talking quietly with Nilda and Kara.

Then I looked for Roarr, but he was standing practically at my elbow.

"Who is it?" I asked.

"A girl named Brana—" Thorge started to say.

But I cut him off with a gasp. "Not Fulla's friend?"

"Indeed, I do believe we are thinking of the same girl," Thorge said. "She was last seen outside Haraldr's house, with the girl Fulla. They were both heading towards the council hall."

"That's within eyeshot of Haraldr's front door," Thormund said.

"Fulla reached it," Thorge said. "But Brana did not."

"You were the first on the scene?" I asked, my eyes darting from Thorge to Roarr and back again.

"Not even," Thorge said.

"We were north, by the great tree," Roarr said.

I knew the tree he meant. It stood just outside of the Thors' front door. It was at the very northern edge of the village, on top of the very peak of the hill. Nothing beyond it but the wilds of the forest and the road to Old Norway.

"If anyone was still holding suspicions of you, this should alleviate them, I should think," Thormund said. I couldn't help but notice the way his hands tightened on the shaft of his spear at his words. Like if anyone should attempt to voice more suspicions of Roarr now, they'd have Thormund to deal with.

"He never left my sight, I swear it," Thorge said.

"I believe you," I said.

Roarr said nothing, but I could feel a glow coming off of him. Our show of confidence in him was giving him all the feelings.

"What now?" Thormund asked me.

"Who was the closest patrol to Fulla?" I asked.

"That would be us," Nilda said as she joined our group. Kara had moved around to the other side to stand beside her husband.

But Esja was still standing by the well, talking with her friend Sigvin. And I couldn't help feeling like that had been a deliberate action on the part of the Mikkelsens. Or, at least, Nilda. She wanted to speak to me without Esja overhearing, or even noticing that she was being spoken about.

"What did you see?" I asked.

"We got there too late, I fear," Nilda said. "Brana was already gone. We came across Fulla alone, searching for her friend in every dark corner. She said they had been walking together, hand in hand. But then Brana's hand slipped from hers, and when Fulla turned to find out why, Brana simply wasn't there."

"Where's Fulla now?" I asked, looking around the square.

"She's with Haraldr and Brigida," Kara said.

Along with Valki, Haraldr and Brigida were the council of three that ruled Villmark. And they had guards around them, in the council hall. Fulla couldn't possibly be in safer hands.

"She was very upset," Nilda said, as if she felt like she had to explain why she hadn't brought the girl to me.

"Of course she is," I said. "You did the right thing. I can call on her later, if I feel I have to."

"But how is Esja?" Roarr asked. Apparently, he, too, had noticed the way the Mikkelsens had elected to leave her behind when joining our conversation.

"Esja is…" Kara started, but apparently words just failed her.

"She left our side," Nilda said, pitching her voice so low I could barely catch what she was saying. "Just before we found Fulla, and only for a moment."

"But it was the opportune moment," Kara added grimly.

"It truly only was a moment," Nilda insisted. "We had just noticed she wasn't with us when we heard Fulla whisper-calling for her friend. By the time we reached Fulla's side, Esja was back with us."

"Exploring more shadows?" I asked.

"We didn't even bother to ask her this time," Kara said. "I looked at her deeply, though. You know, with my magical sight."

"In the middle of the street?" I asked. Because the last time she had attempted to use her magical vision on Esja, she had been struck with such severe headaches that she had been all but blinded, nauseous enough to vomit more than once. She had been forced to lie quietly in the darkness for hours before she recovered.

Of course, whatever was in Esja now wasn't altering her behavior like the last one had.

Or, at least, it was altering it less. And more benignly.

"I didn't see anything wrong with her," Kara said. "She's perfectly normal. Perfectly Esja."

"Yes, but we've been down this road before, haven't we?" I grumbled.

"She looks normal now," Roarr said, but in a small voice.

"She does," I agreed.

But I knew with Esja and whatever entity was stalking her, that really meant nothing at all.

"I have to take her to my grandmother," I said. "And I don't think I can wait until morning to do it."

"I'll come with you," Roarr volunteered.

"No," I said. "Stay here, in town. Thormund, we need to get these patrols moving again. It's possible that Brana, like Disa, is still here to be found."

"Probably not," Thormund sighed. "But I can see the wisdom in not letting everyone give up so quickly. I'll get them moving."

"And I'll look for clues," Roarr said. "Or what clues I can find without your skills."

"I'll be back," I said. "As soon as I can, I'll be back."

But even as I walked over to where Esja was talking with Sigvin, I already knew in my bones.

As soon as I could was not going to be soon enough at all.

CHAPTER EIGHT

WE REACHED the back door to the mead hall just as my grandmother
was closing down for the night. A few straggling Villmarkers were
just coming out as we waited to go in.

But only a very few. In fact, just three men.

Beyond the building and past the stands of dense pine trees, the
sky to the east over the lake was just beginning to turn a lighter shade
of blue.

I watched the three men stumble past, heading for the steep path
up the bluff to the cavern behind the waterfall. It was a treacherous
walk even if you hadn't been up all night downing mug after mug of
my grandmother's sweet, but strong, mead.

Not that I offered to help. They had chosen to spend the night here
when nearly everyone else in Villmark was also staying up all night,
but patrolling for the good of the town. I wasn't sure if these few men
hadn't known or hadn't cared.

It was probably better if I didn't know for sure. The answer wasn't
going to be one I liked much.

Esja followed me into the mead hall without a word. The interior was darker than usual, as my grandmother had snuffed out
most of the lanterns and braziers around the room, and the fire in

the grand fireplace had burned down to dull red embers. The floor was sticky with spilled mead and beer and liberally dusted with food crumbs.

But all of that would magically reset without my grandmother lifting a finger as soon as the sun fully rose. And the tables would be scrubbed clean, and the chairs stacked neatly away.

And then, when the first rays of dawn reached the Runde side of the building, all of this would change from mead hall to municipal center. There would be a bar with rickety folding tables and faded plastic chairs under recently replaced ceiling tiles, so at least the water stains were gone now.

And beyond that would be a cozy little grocery store, and a nook in the far wall that served as post office for all the residents of Runde.

But my grandmother no longer ran that part of things. Now that she was feeling her age—ha! She was more than a hundred but looked like she was still sixty—she was entrusting the daytime Runde activities to two of the Swanson boys. Well, they were young men now, but still all too prone to boyish behavior. Working for my grandmother was community service, but at least it was work they were undertaking without too much grumbling.

My grandmother really needed the break from being everything to everyone in two separate towns.

But that thought only made me feel more guilty for turning up right at closing time with a big problem.

Although it was scarcely surprising after I had led Esja through the main drinking and dining area to the bar where my grandmother served up her mead to find my grandmother standing in the doorway between the two rooms, apparently waiting for us.

She was dressed in her usual Runde clothes of faded jeans, battered work boots, and brightly new flannel shirt rolled up to her elbows. Her long silver hair hung in a thick braid down her back and swung with the motion of her head as she tipped it to one side to give us both a mildly quizzical look.

"I've heard about the fire," she said as she crossed her arms over her chest. "I rather expected you to come to me a bit sooner."

"Sorry. It was a busy night," I said. "Has anyone filled you in on the disappearances?"

"Yes," she said. Then she narrowed her eyes at me. "You think they're related?"

"I don't know what to think," I admitted. I wanted to throw up my hands in frustration. I wanted to burst into tears.

But mainly, I wanted to curl up in bed and sleep for a day and a half. Not that that was in the cards.

"What about you?" my grandmother asked Esja. "Do you know what to think?"

Esja pondered the glib question seriously. "I feel like me. But then again, I felt like me before. I've been letting the others decide when I'm not myself. Roarr has been watching me."

"But not seeing anything," my grandmother said, with her usual astute ability at guessing correctly.

"There was a moment this night when Roarr was being considered a suspect by some of the others," I said. "Not me, but some of the other Villmarkers out on patrol. It was necessary to put them in separate groups for a few hours."

"And his name has now been cleared?" my grandmother guessed.

"Yes. Another girl was taken. Fulla's friend, Brana, disappeared from the front steps of the council hall. Roarr was with Thorge at the time, very near Valki's house," I said.

"So nowhere near the scene of the crime," my grandmother said. But her eyes were on Esja. And they were examining the girl with an intensity I knew meant she was gazing not just in the visual spectrum but also in the magical one.

"Esja was with the Mikkelsens," I said. "But twice she moved away from them. Only for a moment. But at least the second time, there remains a possibility that she was gone from the Mikkelsens at the same moment that Brana was taken."

"Wait, I'm here because you think I'm a suspect?" Esja said, appalled.

"If Ingrid had brought you here because of what happened at the fire, she would've done so much sooner," my grandmother said.

I didn't miss the chastisement in those words that she was throwing my way. Even if she was still gazing fixedly at Esja.

"I'm guessing you don't see anything," I said. "Roarr and I haven't either."

My grandmother made a humming sound, but it was a dismissive one.

"I was only trying to help," Esja said, hugging herself in a way that made all the valkyrie aura she had been carrying around her all night just fade away. She was once more a sickly shut-in, forced to rely too much on the kindness of others.

"How were you helping?" my grandmother asked. But not in a mean way. More like she was genuinely interested.

"I kept sensing things," Esja said, although she sound irritated even saying the words out loud. "Just my imagination, I know now. But in the moment, I really thought I was feeling something."

"Feeling, not seeing?" I asked.

"I would see shadows out of the corner of my eye," Esja said, her tone speculative before turning to self-directed anger again. "*Maybe.*"

"What did you feel?" I asked her. The earnestness of my words seemed to get through to her, and she looked at me with wide, startled eyes.

"Did *you* feel something?" she asked me.

But I just shook my head at her. "No, you first. What did you feel?"

"It was cold," she said, half closing her eyes as if she was working to summon the memory of the sensation. "It was like a cold in my bones, you know? And it moved up the lane to me. Both times, it was like it was moving. But it wasn't just the wind."

"No, not a wind," I said, but she didn't seem to hear me.

"The wind chills your skin, right? And you can feel it in your hair and on your clothes. This wasn't that. This was like something moved up the lane and passed through my insides. I felt it in the marrow of my bones."

She shivered as if at the memory and hugged herself all the tighter.

My grandmother's eyes were on me now.

I shrugged. "That's a perfect description, actually."

"You felt it too?" Esja asked miserably.

"Only the once," I said.

"When we thought Disa was gone, right? It was right before the scream," she said.

"Yes," I said. "It must've passed up the lane, through you and then through me and Thormund." Then I looked over at my grandmother. "Thormund felt it too."

My grandmother nodded that she was noting this piece of information.

"But you felt it twice?" I asked Esja.

"Yes, the second time was near the council hall," she said. "I felt it, but it wasn't moving south to north this time. It was coming down a cross street, from west to east. I turned when I felt it to see if I could see… anything. Anything at all."

"But there was nothing to be seen," I guessed.

"I didn't wander off," she said almost defensively. "I only turned to look. But Nilda and Kara hadn't felt anything at all. They had just kept on walking. They had left me behind."

"Kara was watching you in particular," I said. But it was kind of a question.

"She was," Esja said, but slowly, as if she were consulting her memories again. "I think that cold…. whatever. It disrupted her focus. Just for an instant, but she didn't notice that she had stopped watching me."

I exchanged a long look with my grandmother, but she had no answers for me, I could tell.

"Then we heard Fulla trying to call out to Brana without speaking above a whisper. I was right behind them when they found her. I didn't wander off," she said again. Not quite sullenly, but close.

"Esja needs sleep," my grandmother said to me.

I just shrugged. The whole town needed sleep.

"I see nothing around her, but then I didn't last time."

There was just an edge to those words, like my grandmother was annoyed with herself. And I realized that when she had grumbled before about my not bringing Esja to see her right after the fire, it was because she thought I didn't think I had needed her in that moment.

That certainly *hadn't* been what I was thinking. I had been thinking more about all my grandmother already did, maintaining all the magic that kept her mead hall thriving yet invisible to the outside world.

I hadn't wanted to bother her. But that absolutely didn't mean I didn't think I needed her.

"I was wondering, maybe it would be better for Esja to stay here in Runde, with you," I said.

"Here?" my grandmother repeated.

"Well, in your cabin," I said.

My grandmother had rebuilt her cabin as an almost exact replica of her last cabin. She had meticulously replicated every detail. Including the cozy little room at the top of the stairs with its cozy little built-in bunk. That had been my bedroom as a child, and then again when I'd returned to the north after spending more than a decade in St. Paul.

I wondered if Esja would love that space as much as I always had. The bunk felt like being on a ship having a nautical adventure. And every morning I could sit up and look out the little window in the bunk's back wall. Between two stands of pines, Lake Superior was just visible. And while it was long past the time of year when the sun rose northerly enough to be visible from that window, the view was still breathtaking every single day.

Esja looked from me to my grandmother and back again with nervous excitement in her blue eyes. She had been to the mead hall more than once in the last month, but she had never been outside the doors into Runde proper.

As anxious as my grandmother made her, the idea of living in Runde, even if just for a little while, had real appeal for her.

But my grandmother was already shaking her head. "No, I don't think that would be wise."

"I can help out," Esja said. "I can't really cook, but Ingrid lets me do some of the cleaning around her house. She says I do a good job. Don't you, Ingrid?"

I didn't quite know what to say to that. I had assigned Esja some housekeeping chores, as well as Roarr, more in keeping with the idea that roommates shared the responsibility for such things. The idea that I was "letting" her do mundane chores was a new one to me.

But I saw Esja was starting to droop, assuming there was another reason for my lack of response.

"She's very diligent," I rushed to say, and she perked up again.

But my grandmother just shook her head another time. "Look, it's clear to me that whatever happened at the fire, it awakened something in Esja. Something decidedly of her family's valkyrie line."

"I didn't even know we had a valkyrie line," Esja said.

"Through your mother, you do," my grandmother told her.

"Thormund said something similar, actually," I said. "I just thought it was because she was wearing clothes like the Mikkelsens."

"No, there's more to it than that," my grandmother said. "I don't think we need to worry much about our Esja anymore. Although weapons practice with Nilda and Kara is definitely in order."

"I've been doing that," Esja said. Which was news to me. But at my questioning look, she flushed red. "Not with the Mikkelsens. I meant, I've been doing that with Roarr. And sometimes Skefill. When he visits."

Which was *definitely* news to me.

But to my surprise, my grandmother just chuckled at my gaping expression.

"Villmark looks after its own," she told me, patting my arm affectionately. "It's not all on you, even though you seem to prefer to feel that way."

"I don't," I insisted.

But Esja's eyes were laughing at me. "You kind of do."

I scowled at her.

"I *am* glad you came down to see me," my grandmother said. "I like to see things with my own eyes," she added with a darting look towards Esja. But then she was directing her attention at me again. "You both look absolutely beat. You should get some sleep while you can. Whatever is happening up in Villmark, you haven't solved it yet.

But there's little to be done by the light of day when trouble comes in the dark of night. Get some sleep."

She gave me a quick hug, then shooed us both out of her mead hall.

I looked over at Esja as the magical light behind us lulled down to its soft daytime glow, even as the light from the rising sun found more and more gaps through the tree cover to reach us.

I guessed I could see it, what everyone else was seeing. It was like she was taller, stronger.

But also, kind of golden?

And the hand she was resting on the hilt of her new sword had a capable quality to it.

But even as she gave me a brilliant smile before heading up the trail home, I felt a stab of sadness.

She looked so good, so healthy, so confident.

But she was so changed, I wasn't even sure her brother would recognize her, when he came back to town.

And I really didn't know what he would think.

CHAPTER NINE

I SLEPT through until nearly dinnertime. No one had knocked on my door all day, although my dreams were permeated with the murmur of voices passing by on the road outside my bedroom window, the twittering of birds in my neighbor's tree, and the smell of dried plant detritus thick in the air from someone doing a last cleanup of their garden at the end of the growing season.

I might have kept sleeping forever if other smells hadn't worked their way into my dream world. Eggs frying in butter. Chicken and apple sausage browning on a cast-iron pan. The subtler scents of bread darkening into toast.

The overwhelming aroma of bacon frying up crisp.

I dressed as quickly as I could and ran downstairs to find Esja and Roarr both at work in the kitchen. Roarr was manning the stove, frying the eggs in one pan while the bacon and sausage occupied different halves of my largest cast-iron griddle. Esja had been relegated to making the toast, cutting a loaf of bread fresh from the market into thin, even slices, before setting them in groups of four inside my toaster oven.

But they weren't alone. Mjolner was there too, licking his paw in a way that told me he'd manage to sneak a bit of something tasty when no one was watching. I just hoped it wasn't a swipe from the butter dish. Again.

And on the far side of the kitchen, filling mug after mug with coffee that had just finished brewing, was Thormund.

"Well met, Ingrid," he said as he handed one of the mugs to me. "Esja and Roarr tell me that you caught up on much-needed sleep. That is good."

"Was I needed?" I asked.

"No, but my father asked me to bring you up to date with matters of the council," he said. He tipped his head towards the table, and I joined him there. I saw the butter was still neatly covered, so Mjolner must have snagged something else.

I reached for the little pitcher of cream and added a healthy dollop to my coffee. "What has the council been up to?" I asked at last.

"They have agreed to institute a curfew," he said. "No one is to be out of doors after sunset, save for those on patrol. And we've formalized the rank structure for those. It's not much you need to burden yourself with. Just know that my father will know where every person out tonight is at any given point. If anyone should go missing again, we'll be able to account for every single person on patrol. No one is going anywhere alone."

"Were people alone last night?" Esja asked as she brought a plate stacked high with golden toast over to the table and sat down with us.

"You were," I pointed out.

"And Roarr was, however briefly," Thormund said. "But you weren't the only two who wandered off from their groups. My father's attempts to get an idea of who might have been in the area when Brana disappeared have been thwarted again and again."

"So the council was questioning all the patrols from last night about what they saw?" I asked, sitting back so that Roarr could slide a plate loaded with eggs and meat in front of me. He set a plate twice the size of mine in front of Thormund, who dug in with a hearty appetite.

"That was the intention, but he abandoned it early on when it was proving so fruitless," Thormund said between mouthfuls of egg. "The hope is that if something should happen again tonight—which seems likely—more information can be gleaned with the precautions he's taken."

"That makes sense," I said. "Everyone knows what they are accountable for. Which is watching each other as much as hunting for whoever is abducting people."

"I'll stay close," Esja said. "If I think I see something, I'll say something to you before I go charging after it."

"That would be best," Thormund said. "Roarr, you will be with Thorge again tonight."

"Of course," Roarr said, coming back with plates for him and Esja. Then we all were quiet, at least for the few minutes it took us to demolish all that food as well as a second pot of coffee.

The light coming in from the windows in my living room was losing its golden tone, and I knew that we were nearing sunset. Working together, we made quick work of the dishes. Then the others gathered their weapons, and I double-checked my supplies in my art bag.

Sketchbook, pencils and charcoal sticks, magic wand. All set.

Then we went out to join the general mustering in the village commons. This time, the families with young children were already inside the council hall. All that remained in the square were the volunteers for the patrols. A thinner crowd than the night before, but everyone save me were armed. And we all shared the same determined look on our faces.

This night, we had to catch the culprit. We were prepared, and we would not fail. That was our common if unspoken mission.

Thormund and Thorge helped their father get all the various groups organized and sent on their way. Then Thorge and Roarr joined the Mikkelsens heading due west first.

And Thormund led Esja and me due south.

"I thought we should check the area where Brana was last seen first," he told me as we walked past the closed doors and shuttered windows of the marketplace. "Perhaps you would like to try drawing the area. See what you can see."

"Very much so," I said. I didn't admit out loud that I had intended to do that during the day, but had slept far too late instead.

We stopped at the bottom of the steps up to the large, double wooden doors of the council hall. They were closed, so snug that not even a glimmer of light revealed the fact that there were dozens of people gathered within.

"It was more over here," Esja said, leading the way into the darkness along the side of the building. There was a thicket of dried shrubs, the ground beneath them littered with the remains of crumbling leaves. "Just here," she said, stopping in a gap between two of the shrubs. "There's something like a walking path through here. It winds around the back of that house there, then ends in a side gate into Haraldr's garden."

"Why didn't they stick to the road?" I wondered aloud. But I didn't expect either of my companions to have an answer. I just sat down in the dust and dried grass and took out my sketchbook.

I slipped in and out of my fugue state with the ease of long experience at this sort of thing. But when I was done, all I had again were pages and pages of drawings of the lake.

"I can smell the lake, I think," Esja said, as if trying to buck up my spirits.

"It's not just the lake," Thormund said from where he had, without asking, taken up a position behind me as I drew.

"What do you mean?" I asked, touching the darkest patch of one of the drawings. I had used charcoal this time, but the heaviness of the lines was the same as I had done the night before with graphite. It just didn't have the same shine to it.

"You're drawing the depths of the lake," he said. "I can feel it, when I look at your drawings. I can feel the cold depths of that lake, the way I sometimes sense it below us when we're out on the longship."

"So it's not just me," I mused.

Then I heard a rustle of leaves and looked up to see Esja disappearing into the denser patch of thicket. It took me a minute to get to my feet, but Thormund reacted faster, charging in after her. They were both gone from sight before I had my charcoal and sketchbook back in my bag and could follow.

But I didn't have far to go. Esja had left the path to charge through the heavier growth of shrubs around the back of the council hall, then out again, back on the main north-south road. Thormund was beside her, spear at the ready in his hands. They were both looking around almost desperately, like they had felt ghostly hands on them and were hunting for the source.

Then I was out of the thicket as well, out onto the cobblestoned road. And I felt it again, that feeling like a wind blowing through my very bones. And it was whipping through me from the south, going uphill to the north. I was sure of it.

"There," Esja said, half in a whisper, as she pointed up towards the village commons. "It's like silvery banners of fairy light, isn't it?"

"You can see it?" I asked, squinting in the direction she was pointing. But I saw nothing at all.

"Yes," Esja said. "It looks like a miniature version of the Northern Lights, but low to the ground and sort of dancing up the road. You don't see it?"

"I see nothing," Thormund said.

"Nor do I," I said.

"I'm not imagining it," Esja said.

"No, I don't think you are," I told her. "I think you're more sensitive to this—whatever it is—than I am. Do you see where it's going?"

"Follow it, and we'll follow you," Thormund said, gesturing with his spear for her to hurry.

Esja gave us both a grim nod, then started jogging up the hill, hand on the hilt of her sword.

We reached a point about a block north of the marketplace when her steps came to a halt and she stood in the middle of the road, pivoting this way and that.

"You lost the trail?" Thormund asked.

"Or it ends here?" I suggested.

Esja chewed at her lip. Then she turned, suddenly, as if at a crash of noise.

Only she did that turn a split second before I even heard the noise. Like she had known it was coming somehow.

"There!" she said, and charged down a darkened lane between two tall fences. Thormund ran after her, then picked up speed to sprint past her. I was following, but nowhere near close enough to see what happened after he turned sharply to the left, following a different perpendicular lane. But I heard someone's startled yelp, then Thormund's muffled curse.

I rounded the corner to find him standing with his hands on his thighs as he caught his breath. Esja was beside him, scanning our surroundings. But we were in a lane between two fences. There was nothing to see but a few scattered leaves.

"Did he get away?" I asked.

"It's too dark in here," Esja grumbled. "I think he jumped that fence. But then I think he jumped three more fences. There's no catching him now."

"Who was it?" I asked.

"Too dark," Thormund said, still breathing hard from his burst of speed. "Too fast."

"I should've been quicker," Esja said, her hands in futile fists. "I sensed him, but not fast enough. He got away."

"Did the wind lead you to him? Or was it just blowing past him?" I asked.

"That's what I want to know," Thormund said. "Did I just fail to hold on to our culprit? Or was it merely someone shirking the curfew order?"

I looked at Esja. I could see her face working as she pondered what she had sensed. But she gave in with a shrug.

"I think, could be either?" she said. "The wind was definitely heading north, and this guy hiding in the lane was not. But if he knew I was on to him, he might've been trying to misdirect me."

"Or maybe you thwarted his current attempt at an abduction," I said. "I think you did, before. With Disa."

"I did?" she said, blinking at me in surprise.

"We both felt the wind," Thormund said. "But no one was taken. If whoever is doing this knows you can sense them, you might be disrupting his plans."

"If only for a moment," I said. "He still got Brana."

"We need to patrol more," Esja said. "I need to cover more ground, right?"

I exchanged a look with Thormund. I could tell we were sharing the same thought. It was great that Esja wanted to help out, and maybe she could be our best resource in tracking this guy.

But if he knew she could catch him, she was in even more danger than she knew.

But I didn't want to tell her. She was so eager to be of use, after a lifetime of being cared for by others.

"We should cover more ground," Thormund said, then gestured for her to lead the way.

But he shot another look at me the instant her back was turned. We both had to watch out for her.

I really hated the idea that we were using Esja as bait, but it was hard not to think of it that way.

But we would be better prepared the next time we got close, I just knew it.

We had to be.

CHAPTER TEN

WE SPENT the whole night criss-crossing the entirety of Villmark, but the only thing to ever cross our path were other groups out on patrol. We never felt that bone-chilling non-wind again.

We didn't catch another glimpse of the shadowy figure that Esja and Thormund had chased through the lanes.

But we also didn't lose anyone. When the sun rose over the lake and all the patrols gathered again at the village commons, no one had anything to report. But we already knew that everyone in town was accounted for.

Valki's chain of command wasn't just a matter of organizing the patrols. He had set up neighborhood groups. Before the sun had completely cleared the eastern horizon, he definitively knew that everyone in town was present and accounted for.

Which I suppose was good news. Esja really had thwarted that night's attempt at abduction, although who the target might have been wasn't exactly clear.

But it felt like a hollow victory. We all dragged ourselves back home to bed, to catch what sleep we could before doing it all over again the next night.

I curled up with Mjolner at the back of my neck and slipped into that same fog of daytime sleeping, where my dreams were all tangled up with the sounds I could hear through my bedroom windows. The rattle of passing carts, the running and laughing of children at play, the barking of dogs.

But I didn't sleep all the way until dinnertime. Although waking to the smells of breakfast would've been infinitely preferable to another pounding at the door.

This time, it was my bedroom door that was being knocked on. And to be fair, it was a light knock meant not to wake me if I were deeply asleep. An inquiring kind of knock, but a persistent one.

I got out of bed to find Roarr at my door, already dressed for the night's patrol. But a quick glance at my watch showed that was still hours away.

"I have something to tell you," he said.

"Am I going to have something to do after you tell me?" I asked with a large yawn.

"Definitely yes," he said.

"Then let me get dressed," I sighed.

I had gotten enough sleep, at least by a measure of hours. But it hadn't felt restful. I didn't feel recharged.

Not that I had any choice. I knew from the look on Roarr's face that what he had to tell me was both serious, and something he had already decided he couldn't just deal with on his own.

It was going to take a volva, whatever it was. And these days, that was just me.

At least when I made it back down the stairs, it was to find a fresh pot of coffee waiting for me, as well as a tray of cinnamon buns that just had to have come from my grandmother. It was such a welcome sight, I almost wanted to cry.

She couldn't come up to Villmark to help me because the mead hall was her focus now. But she was still thinking of me.

I devoured four buns and half a mug of coffee before finally looking up at Roarr, who was anxiously watching me eat.

"Go," I said.

"I heard a rumor last night that some young men were intending to violate the curfew," he said. "They took a boat out to go fishing, but that was just an excuse. The real reason was just to thumb their noses at authority."

"A rumor, so someone on the patrols knew about this, but no one went to Valki about it?" I asked with a frown.

"There wouldn't have been any proof," Roarr said. "This chain of command that Valki set up to keep people accountable has one big flaw."

"What's that?" I asked as I pulled apart another cinnamon bun.

"It assumes everyone will be honest," he said.

"So these young men out on the boat reported to someone who was willing to lie for them, or cover up what they were really doing," I said.

"It's my fault," Roarr said, his cheeks flushing darkly.

"How could that possibly be true?" I asked.

"Because the ones behind this are Raggi and Skefill. They've gotten their gang all riled up, and they're doing this to prove a point," Roarr said.

"Because Thorge cleared your name?" I said. "Is that why this is your fault?"

"They liked me better as a suspect," he said with a shrug that wasn't nearly as careless as he wanted it to appear.

"Okay," I said, pulling my bun apart into smaller and smaller fragments as I pondered. "We did formally clear you of suspicion, sure. But the fact of the matter is, you're still patrolling with Thorge. Who is still watching every move you make, the same as when you were considered a suspect. So what's their objection?"

"I honestly don't know," he said. "But I'm not being paranoid. They really don't like me. And not even because of what Halldis made me do. It goes back further than that."

I gathered up bits of cinnamon bun and munched on them as I thought that over. I was pretty sure he was right. Raggi and Skefill went out of their way to let everyone know how little they thought of Roarr.

And now that he'd said so, I realized he was right. The fact that he had been used as a tool by the witch Halldis, that she had manipulated him into fetching magical items for her that she had no business possessing, that she had coerced him into helping her cover up crimes all the way up to murder, none of that was what Raggi and Skefill actually couldn't forgive him for.

Because, although she had come from the north, Halldis had been one of them, a descendant of the original settlers that Torfa had brought over from Norway.

But Roarr, since he was a teenager, had loved a girl from Runde. And he had been preparing to leave Villmark to live a life with her out in the world beyond Runde. My world. The world the two of them as isolationists wanted nothing to do with.

"I keep seeing the lake," I mused as I used a fingertip to blot up the last crumbs of cinnamon and sugar. "Every time I try to draw what is happening here, I see the lake. But I don't think that means Runde."

"These guys took a boat out onto the lake last night," Roarr said. "Is that related, or just a coincidence?"

"I want to say coincidence," I said. "Esja felt something last night. Well, I did too, but she felt it clearer than I did. And Thormund almost caught someone. Although Esja wasn't sure if he was the culprit, or just someone lurking in the dark. If people are being encouraged to violate the curfew, they might not all be doing it out on the lake. On the other hand, if whatever is happening *does* involve the lake, maybe going out at night to fish disrupted things."

"We could take the longship out," Roarr suggested.

"Maybe," I said. "But the lake is huge, and I don't even know what we'd be looking for."

"I could go down to the harbor behind the waterfall and make sure the ship is ready to get underway in case we do need it," Roarr said.

"Why do I feel like you know I have to go talk to Valki next, and you'd do anything not to be there when I do?" I asked. I was teasing, but the returning flush to his cheeks told me I had hit the mark.

"You can tell me again and again that this isn't my fault, but it still feels like it is," he said. "Even volunteering for the nightly patrols isn't getting me back in anyone's good graces. I don't know what will."

"Time," I told him, and downed the last of my coffee in one long swallow. "It's just going to take some time. Now, I *do* have to go see Valki. But Esja is still sleeping?"

"No, I'm up," Esja said as she came into the kitchen, scratching at her sleep-twisted braids. She made a beeline to the coffee, but then said, "Give me a minute to wake up, then I'll go with you to check on the longship, Roarr."

"After that, why don't you hook up with the Mikkelsens for a little sword practice before patrolling?" I suggested.

"Sword practice? Is that what we call babysitting these days?" Esja said. But she was quick to add, "Not that I'm objecting. I can stay with them until patrol time and then be back with you and Thormund tonight."

"Sorry to foist you off on Nilda and Kara, but I do need Roarr," I said.

"You do?" Roarr asked, surprised.

"I could take Thormund or Thorge with me, I suppose, but I suspect that when I'm done talking to Valki, they're both going to be quite busy indeed redoing all of Valki's chains of command before sunset," I said.

"So you need me for what exactly?" he asked.

Not that I could blame him for sounding apprehensive. I doubted he was going to like the task at hand any better than I did. But it had to be done.

"We're going to go talk to Raggi about what he's been up to," I said. "And then, after him, we'll do the same with Skefill. I hope you're up for it."

"They can hate me all they like," Roarr said. "I'm as much a Vill-marker as they are. And what they're doing hurts Villmark. They'll answer your questions, if I have anything to say about it."

"I think they know the drill by now," I said. "Meet me at Valki's house when you're done with the longship, and we'll head to Raggi's house."

"Great," Roarr said with a distinct lack of enthusiasm.

For my part, I was actually a little curious. I had never seen Raggi's house before. The times I had questioned him before had always been in Aldis' mead hall or some similar public place.

I guessed I was about to find out how a "true" Villmarker lived.

CHAPTER ELEVEN

VALKI TOOK what I had to tell him about as well as I had expected him to. By which I mean, not well at all.

For a minute, I worried he was just going to charge out and find Raggi and Skefill and the other young men they'd been leading astray, and then start smashing heads together. I mean, worried in a "I kind of want to see this" kind of way.

But in the end, his wife Gunna convinced him that breaking up his reporting hierarchy would be the better plan all around. The trouble-makers would be mixed in with the trustworthy patrollers, but since the troublemakers were so few, the swing of influence would have to be towards the side of good.

I certainly hoped so. But in the short-term, this meant that the Mikkelsens were going to be split up that night, each patrolling with a different group of men who may or may not be trying to sneak in some night fishing if the opportunity should present itself.

And Thorge himself was going to be patrolling with Raggi and Skefill. Which meant that Roarr would be joining me and Esja and Thormund.

Although that had come after a long discussion about making Roarr sit out patrolling. But putting him on guard duty with the young families inside of the council hall wasn't going to fool anyone. Everyone in Villmark would take it as a sign that Roarr had no one's trust.

Because it *would* be a sign of just that.

I had to argue hard to keep him by my side on my patrol. And when Valki finally gave in, I was still wondering why I was arguing so hard for it.

But the truth was, he had my trust. He had worked hard for it over the course of a year, but in the end—and especially with everything he'd done for Esja—he had earned it.

I hadn't realized this was true, and was still feeling a little stunned by that revelation when I went back out into the late afternoon sun, blinking at the golden light that lit up the trees behind the silhouette of Roarr, waiting there at the gate for me to emerge from Valki's house.

"You know where we're going?" I asked him as I adjusted the strap of my art bag a little higher on my shoulder.

"West of town, in the hills just beyond Aldis's mead hall," Roarr said, already leading the way back south to the village commons. From there we took the western road, past Aldis's mead hall.

There were still a couple of hours of sunlight left in the day, but the village around us was remarkably quiet. Like everyone was already withdrawing from the streets, closing up their houses, doing all they could to keep safe through another long, uncertain night.

"We have to solve this thing," I grumbled to myself.

But Roarr heard me. He just said, "We will."

Then we walked in a friendly silence, each lost in our own thoughts, until Roarr nudged my elbow and pointed to the side of a hill just to the north of the road up ahead of us.

Like Aldis's mead hall, this was a version of a sod house, although where her building was fronted by an A-frame wooden structure, this was all stone save the heavy door and the shutters on the window. The sod roof was a mix of prairie grasses, dried now, but with such a variety of structures I rather wished I could see it again in full summer bloom. I would bet the colors were remarkable.

Roarr knocked briskly on the door, then stepped back so that I was the one that Raggi saw first when he eventually answered the door. He was shirtless and barefoot in pants he'd clearly just pulled on, as the fastening in the front wasn't quite done up yet.

He scowled at me, but not in a way that said he hadn't expected to see me.

"Can I come in?" I asked him.

"Let me guess. You have some questions for me," he said. But he just stepped back, leaving the door open behind him. That was as much of an invitation as I was likely to get.

I stepped into the darkness of his shuttered little house, to find at once that it wasn't just *his* little house. Three other men were inside, sleeping in bunks against the far wall. They were each wrapped in blankets or cloaks with their backs turned towards the door, so all I saw were three unidentifiable heads of hair that ranged from dark blond to light brown.

"I'm disturbing you," I said.

"We'll be getting up for patrol soon enough," he said.

"So you will be patrolling tonight?" I asked.

"I've patrolled every night," he said in a low growl.

Roarr caught my eye and gave me a little nod.

"You've been patrolling, but you've been letting others shirk their duties, haven't you?" I said.

"Patrol is a volunteer position, last I heard," he said as he poked at the remains of a fire in the fireplace. A cast-iron pot hung low over those coals, filled with what I could only assume was mystery soup. Add an ingredient or two, fill up a bowl for dinner. Repeat the next day, and the next day. Neverending soup.

Not my idea of good cooking, but it *was* traditional. And when he gave it a stir, the smell of meat and potatoes reminded me that cinnamon buns, while tasty, were not really a proper meal.

"No one has to patrol, that's true," I said. "But those who aren't patrolling are meant to check in and report their locations to their neighborhood representatives. That's how the rest of us know everyone is accounted for."

"We don't exactly have a neighborhood out here," Raggi said with a gesture towards the door.

"I know you've been told who to report to," I said mildly. "Or do you want to tell me that isn't true? That Valki was less than thorough?"

Raggi scowled but said nothing as he stirred at his warming soup.

"I know you like to question authority," I said. "You want to answer only to yourself. But we have a community here. That involves certain obligations to keep everyone safe."

"Or what?" Raggi asked. "You'll banish us from the community?"

"That's been done," Roarr put in.

"Skógganger," Raggi said. "Yes, I'm familiar with it."

"Those who break our laws are banished to the forest," Roarr said to me.

"It's not been done in generations," Raggi said. "But if that is the sentence you want to level for such an offense as ours, by all means. I will obey the word of my chieftain."

Roarr scowled fiercely at that, which only confused me further than Raggi's words already had.

But then I realized what he was saying. "There's a council of three, no chieftain," I pointed out.

Raggi just smirked at me.

"We had a chieftain, once," Roarr said. "That's as much of the past as the punishment of skógganger."

"Like putting people into caves behind the waterfall is so much nobler," Raggi sneered.

"No one is sealed in," I said. "Everyone is getting all the help we can give them. But the people have to be safe. It's not a perfect solution, but a balance is always strived for."

"No one is sealed in," he repeated with a quirk of an eyebrow and the hint of a questioning tone.

"Halldis is sealed in, obviously," I admitted. "But she's no mere human who violated a law. She works with and for evil forces that are even now trying to find their way into Villmark."

"Which is the point of the patrols," Roarr said. "We have to stay vigilant."

"Patrolling the streets isn't keeping anything out, is it?" Raggi asked as he took down a ladle and used it to fill a beautifully carved wooden bowl with steaming hot soup.

As if wakened by the umami smells, the other men in the bunks started to stir. But Raggi ignored them, sitting still shirtless at the little table in the center of the room and digging into his bowl with gusto.

"If you aren't going to take your duties of patrol seriously, then you should step aside and let someone else take them on," I said.

"Skefill and I know we can both be trusted, as well as you and the Thors know you can trust this fellow," Raggi said with a nod of his head towards Roarr. "And Skefill trusts his brother and his cousins as well as he trusts me. So Valki's attempt to keep everyone in contact with each other through circles of trust is fulfilled. I knew where everyone was. I never lied when I said that I did."

"You lied by omission," Roarr said. "You knew they weren't indoors per the curfew. You knew they'd taken a fishing boat out onto the lake."

"And I further knew all they were doing was fishing," Raggi said. Then he looked back over his shoulder at one of the three men who were coming out from under the blankets to stretch and scratch in the semidarkness at the back of the room. "Isn't that right, Hafr?"

One of the men stepped forward into the light from the setting sun streaming in through the still open doorway.

"A-yeah," Hafr said, scratching at his bare chest as he eyed Raggi's soup. "We were all together on the boat. No one got out of anyone else's sight, never once the whole night through. And we were all together out on the lake, well away from the streets of Villmark. Anything that happened there, it had nothing to do with us. We were fishing."

"See? Everyone I reported as being accounted for I had, in fact, accounted for," Raggi said. "And unless you have some reason to consider me a suspect—*again*—I think that's really all I have to say to you."

"The patrols are being broken up differently," I told him. "You'll be assigned a new group when we muster in the village commons."

"Why am I not surprised?" Raggi said, scraping at the bottom of his bowl with his spoon.

"Hafr? Will we see you there as well?" I asked.

"There's going to be a stink if you aren't there," Raggi told him in a whisper that carried throughout the entire room. One of the other men in the back of the room chuckled. But Hafr just shrugged.

"We had a good haul last night," he said. "I guess I can take one night off."

"Tomorrow night, there might still be a curfew. That means no leaving town even to fish," I said. "We'll be deciding that on a night by night basis. No one goes out without getting permission first. Is that clear?"

There was a lot of smirking and traded looks, but not a one of them promised to do as I asked.

But it wasn't worth pressing the point. I just gestured for Roarr to follow me back out of the house.

"You're just going to let them do whatever they want?" he asked, half incredulous and half almost annoyed with me.

"I'm not *letting* them do anything," I said. "I don't see much use in extracting a promise none of them intends to keep, and the spell that my mormor can cast to compel people to keep a vow isn't one I know yet."

"But still..." Roarr said, throwing up his hands when words failed him.

"They aren't wrong, though," I said. "If they were out on a boat all night long, all of them together out on the water, none of them could possibly be suspects, could they? They're just... random distractions."

"Same as ever," Roarr said.

Which, I had to agree with. Every time I had suspected Raggi and his ilk of anything, they always turned out not to be the source of the trouble.

But they never made finding the source any easier. No, in fact, they seemed to thrive on making things as hard for me as possible.

And I still had Skefill to talk to before the sun set.

Somehow, I doubted that conversation was going to go any better.

CHAPTER TWELVE

It was a short walk to the house where Skefill lived, on the outskirts of Villmark, but still on actual streets on the western side of the town and not out in the hills like Raggi and his roommates.

It was in the middle of a block, just a little north and east from Aldis's mead hall. From the street, it looked the same as the other houses in the area. But once we were inside the front gate, I found it was a little more old-fashioned than the other homes, more of a country farmhouse despite being built in the town proper. It was painted a deep shade of red with bright white trim around the doors and window frames, and the front entryway was large and inviting, jutting forward out of what otherwise looked almost like a barn roof running perpendicular to us.

I could hear children's voices inside as Roarr and I stepped up onto that porch to knock on the door. At first I thought they were perhaps coming from the house next door, but when a tired-looking woman scarcely older than I was opened the door, I realized the noise was coming from her children. She had a sleeping baby in a sling across her chest, and another toddler with long golden curls was peeking from around her skirts. I couldn't tell if it was a girl or a boy, even though it was wearing nothing but a diaper at the moment, but whichever it was, it was a beautiful child with bright rosy cheeks and serious dark blue eyes.

"We were hoping to speak with Skefill?" I said.

"Oh," she said, looking back over her shoulder towards her kitchen. "He was just here... Oh, yes. He's gone into the back garden with the twins. You can go right through. Don't mind about your shoes; that central hall runs straight back to the other door, and there's simply no keeping that clean with this many little ones running about."

"If you're sure," I said, and pushed my heel back down into the shoe I had already been slipping it out of.

She just gave me a weary smile, then headed back into her kitchen with the baby and the toddler.

"Skefill's sister," Roarr whispered to me. "Her husband runs the blacksmith shop that marks the very west end of the marketplace."

"I've seen it, but I've never been inside," I said.

We had reached the back door, and Roarr pulled it open. Beyond it was a fenced-in back garden, mostly dominated by a pair of apple trees long since picked over. The ground around the tree trunks was roughly paved in flat river stones that showed a variety of muted colors worn smooth by water and time.

Skefill was sitting on a stone bench between the two trees, two boys of about six gathered close on either side of him. They looked like they could be his kids—sharing his blue-gray eyes and wavy dark blond hair—although I supposed they must be his nephews. They were watching intently as he attempted to get a wheel fastened back onto a little toy wooden cart.

It was a cozy little moment that was completely ruined when he happened to glance up and see Roarr and me standing there just outside his back door.

"Here you go," he said to one of the boys after giving the repaired wheel a couple of test spins. "Now go put it up in your room and get into the kitchen for supper. I'll be walking you all down to the council hall when you're through, so no dawdling."

Our presence seemed to make the two boys as shy as their toddler sibling. The one accepted the repaired toy with a murmur of thanks, and the two of them circled Roarr and me with a wide berth before heading into the house.

The minute the door slammed shut behind them, their noise level returned to its former volume as they charged up the stairs with all the thundering of feet of a small army.

"You probably know why we're here," I said as Skefill made a big show of putting his little tools away inside a worn leather work bag.

"Not really," he said. "If it's about Esja, I haven't seen her in days. I've been busy. If it's about the patrols, I don't report to you. If it's not about either... yeah, I don't have a clue. I *do* have things to get done before I head out for the night, though."

"You and Raggi have been allowing other fishermen to go out on their boat despite the curfew," I said. "And you've been lying to the person you *do* report to, and all the way up the chain of command to the council itself. So it *is* my business."

He barked out a single laugh, then got up from the bench to carry his tool bag across the yard to a little shed tucked in the corner that was painted like a replica of the rest of the house. "Apparently the powers that be decided that some people are to be trusted no matter who holds them in suspicion. So we just decided, maybe we can decide too who we trust and who we don't."

"This isn't about me," Roarr said.

"Isn't it, though?" Skefill said. He set the tool bag inside the shed, then pushed the door shut until he heard the latch click. Then he turned to face us both, arms crossed. "Raggi and I decided that we, too, can decide that we can clear people from suspicion just because we had eyes on them when Brana was taken. We haven't let anyone out on the boat that we didn't clear personally."

"Come on," I said. "There were how many men on that boat?"

"Eight," Skefill said.

"There weren't that many men with you on patrol when Brana was taken," I said. "You couldn't possibly have cleared them."

"And I haven't been allowed to come and go as I will," Roarr added. "I can't violate the curfew any more than anyone else can. I still work a patrol with Thorge as my constant watcher. I haven't been cleared of anything."

Skefill just shrugged, unbothered.

"Who are these eight men?" I asked.

"Cousins of mine, all of them," Skefill said. "Two of them were on patrol with Raggi and me when Brana was taken. The other six were together in another group, also far from the council steps when Brana went missing. They all six vouched for each other."

"That isn't the way this is going to work," I said.

"Isn't it? It felt like that's what we were all doing," Skefill said.

"No, and you know it isn't," I said. "And no one was in such dire need of fresh fish last night, either. You and Raggi just did this to prove a point. And you've wrapped up all your cousins into it as well."

"So it's skógganger for the lot of us, then, is it?" he asked with an arched brow.

I simmered in annoyance but said nothing until I had my breathing back under calm control. Still, it was proof they had done all of it deliberately, to be irritating. Even to the point of flaunting the fact that they already knew they were too valuable to be effectively punished in any meaningful way.

"No one is going out tonight," Roarr said. "You're either on patrol or you're indoors. I've already spoken to the harbor guards, and they are doubling their numbers. You'll never manage to sneak a boat out tonight."

"Or wander out into the woods," I added. "Valki is changing up the roster and the routes for all the patrols. You won't be with your buddies, and no one will be sneaking out of town."

"Well, you've got everything all tied up, then, haven't you?" he said with a hint of a sneer.

"It's a waste of resources when we still don't know what's taking people out of our town, out from under our very noses," I said.

"Do any of us really have any chance of figuring that out?" he snapped back. "We can patrol all we like, but whatever this is took Brana when she was holding Fulla's hand. Took her without a sound, without a trace, without a clue. If *you* can't figure it out, what hope do the rest of us have? I mean, how likely is it we'll get lucky and catch it in the act? When Fulla didn't even see anything? It's all futile."

"I'm doing the best I can," I said. Which must have come out more choked-sounding than I thought, to judge from the sudden comforting presence of Roarr's hand on my shoulder. "All I'm getting is images of the lake, over and over again. I don't know what it means. But it's a good bet that it at least means none of us should be actually going out on the lake right now."

Skefill looked shaken by my words. It took me a minute to figure out this was because he believed me. He believed I had a lead, that the lake was dangerous.

And he had just sent eight of his cousins out on its waters without knowing the danger.

"No one is going out on a boat tonight," I said.

"No, no one," he agreed. "I will make sure of it."

"I mean, I already did," Roarr said, but mostly to himself.

"And I want to see all eight of the men who were out on that boat last night," I said. "I need to look into their eyes before they head out on patrols tonight. Volunteering for which is absolutely the least they can do to make it up to Villmark for what they've done."

Skefill shifted his weight from foot to foot but said nothing.

"What is it?" I asked him wearily.

"It's just, it was more like seven men and one boy," he said. "Or, teenager. Young man? He's seventeen."

"A little young for patrols," Roarr told me, as if I might not already be thinking the same thing.

"He can go down to the council hall with the others, then, but I want to see him first," I said. "I'm not kidding around with this, Skefill. I need to see these men. Just long enough to draw their portraits. I need to be sure they aren't involved, maybe in some way they don't even know."

Skefill's eyes shot to Roarr at those words, but when they came back to mine, he just nodded gravely.

Which, fair enough. Roarr was the living example of being used for bad ends. Although whether what was happening now was even similar, I didn't know. I didn't exactly think so. Even when he was the deepest in Halldis' control, he had never been able to flit through the town as a living ghost.

No, something nonhuman was taking our people off the streets. That was becoming more and more clear every night when another disappeared.

But that didn't mean that people who had been out on the lake hadn't seen or experienced something they didn't understand and didn't know was important. Something I could see hanging on them like the remnants of a spell.

Something that could point me in a direction.

It was a long shot, but all we had were long shots.

"I'll be in the village commons," I told him. "Bring your cousins there."

"I will," he said. "As soon as my sister and her children are settled in the council hall. My brother-in-law has been at his forge day and night all week. Lots of people needing weapons brought back up to usable condition, you know?"

Yeah, I could believe it. Even in Villmark, where everyone liked to think of themselves as living relics from the Viking Age, long years of peace in town had made all of us complacent.

But that time had come to an end. The need for swords and bows was being felt once more.

I didn't exactly like it. But I couldn't argue that it wasn't needed.

Roarr and I ducked back out of the house to see the sun already halfway gone behind the tree-covered hills to the west. The day was ending, and the night was upon us.

And the deepening shadows were making me far more nervous than I liked. Soon I would be like Esja, jumping at everything.

Although, frankly, I wasn't convinced that what Esja was jumping at was *nothing*.

I quickened my steps to get back to the village commons.

CHAPTER THIRTEEN

By the time Roarr and I reached the village commons, there were already crowds of people milling in groups. Valki, Thormund and Thorge were circulating, trying to catch the individuals they had selected to be patrol leaders and then help those leaders round up their assigned patrols.

This was going to take longer than usual, and my edginess only increased the more apparent that became.

What if things started happening right after sunset this time? We would be caught unprepared.

"Come on," Roarr said to me, guiding me by my elbow to one of the benches that bracketed the old well in the center of the square. "I'll go find those cousins and bring them to you. You just sit here and draw. If I can keep them coming without interruption, maybe you won't lose your flow."

"That's a good idea," I said. "Thanks. When you bring them to me, just ask them to tell me everything they remember about last night. And not to worry if I don't respond."

"Sure. I've been on the other end of that before," he said.

I sat down on the bench and put my art bag on the ground by my feet. Then I felt something hop up beside me, a warm furriness pressing against my hip.

"Hey, Mjolner," I said. "Good of you to join us this time."

He meowed at me softly, then curled up to go back to sleep.

Which either meant nothing of import was about to happen, or that he sensed something *huge* was going to happen and he wanted to be fully rested and prepared when it did.

I really missed Loke. He understood Mjolner better than I did. I was sure if Loke was there, he would know which Mjolner meant.

But I was on my own.

I sharpened my charcoal sticks with a scrap of sandpaper and fretted a bit over the growing darkness. The square was ringed with the low LED lights, but none of them were in the middle where I was sitting by the well.

But maybe the darkness would help, since when I was in a fugue state, I wasn't really seeing the paper, anyway.

I looked up at the sound of footsteps coming my way to see not Roarr as I had expected but Skefill. He had two young men with him, one looking sullen and the other looking distraught, like he really didn't want to go to the principal's office and he already regretted breaking the rules. Or, at least, getting caught breaking the rules.

I motioned for the sullen one to sit down on the other end of the bench first.

"Roarr gave us your instructions already," Skefill told me. "I'm just here to make sure they are carried out."

And he gave the sullen young man a fierce glare until that young man finally broke down into something a little closer to contrition.

"Right, we went out in our fishing boat just around midnight," he said.

"Every detail you can remember, please," I said even as I put charcoal pencil to paper.

Despite that prompting, the first man only gave me the broadest strokes of the expedition. He couldn't remember what the weather was like, which for a fisherman felt really odd, but I let it pass. He couldn't remember anything in particular about the other men on the boat.

He did have an exact count of the fish that were caught, both by number and by weight, before and after they'd been processed in the fish house after the crew got back to shore.

When he ran out of words, I was vaguely aware of Skefill chasing him away from the bench. Then the contrite fellow was in his place, quickly starting his own version of the story before I had even finished the shading of the last sketch.

I turned the page and started fresh with his more illustrative version of the events. The clear moonless skies, the starlight sparkling on the water. The unusual quiet of the water and the soft rolls of the waves. The silvery shine of the fish in the boat's one artificial light.

The third and fourth men filled in little more than I knew already.

The fifth was musically inclined, and either had been singing the entire time they were out on the water or just preferred to remember it that way. The pencil in my hand traced long flowing lines as if chasing the notes he was singing to me, and I was sure even in my fugue state I was smiling as I drew.

The sixth and the seventh were earnest in their desire to dig deep and find new details. But it had, for the fishermen out on that boat anyway, been a very quiet night.

Then I came out of that fugue state all at once, suddenly aware of the cooler night air on my skin, and the way my eyes were straining to see the dark lines of charcoal on the page before me.

"Is that it?" the man on the other side of the bench asked me anxiously.

"Yeah," I said as I turned back pages in my sketchbook. "Yes. I'm done with you. Thank you, you can rejoin your patrol."

Then I looked up at the sky, but with no moon up there, I didn't have much of a way to gauge the time of night. I mean, technically I knew that the stars moved in predictable ways too. I just had never paid enough attention to know what their positions now meant.

"Here's Fjolnir," Skefill said as he approached. Fjolnir had to be the teenager, since the other seven who had already been on my bench had all been grown men.

But as Skefill pushed the boy out in front of him, I realized he wasn't just *a* teenager. He was practically the poster boy for teenagers. Sullen, stoop-shouldered and gangly, looking down at his toes with his hands deep in his pockets and the overly long locks of his hair falling over his face, hiding his eyes entirely.

Seriously. He was like the Platonic ideal of a moody teenaged boy.

"Fjolnir," I said, gesturing for him to sit on the other end of my bench. He scowled at me. Then, when Skefill nudged his shoulder, he turned to scowl at Skefill.

But, in the end, he took his seat there. Only to sit with his arms crossed, refusing to say a word.

"Let's get this going. My own patrol is waiting for me," Skefill growled at him, but the boy just scowled all the deeper.

"You can go," Roarr offered as he emerged from the shadows on the far side of the well. "Thormund, Esja and I can walk him down to the council hall with Ingrid after she's done."

"Yes, I did want to visit Fulla, and I understand she's there," I said.

"If you're sure," Skefill said.

"We've got it," I said.

Skefill nodded briskly. Then he put a hand on Fjolnir's shoulder, leaning down to whisper something in the boy's ear. Fjolnir said nothing, just jerked away from the touch as Skefill backed away.

Roarr also melted back into the shadows. I suspected he had been there the entire time I had been sketching the others, watching without interfering.

I traded out my charcoal stick for a fresher one, turned to a blank page in my sketchbook, then looked up at Fjolnir expectantly.

"I don't have to tell you anything," he said.

"No, at this point, I think I've got all the details," I agreed cheerily. "I mean, what could you have seen that the others didn't see?"

He opened his mouth as if to contradict me, then thought better of it and closed it again without a word.

But I started sketching anyway. He was vibrating with unexpressed feelings, and I was very attuned to it. I had been a moody teen myself, not so long ago. It didn't take much to remember that feeling, like none of the grownups would really understand.

I was drawing the lake again. I knew that on some level.

And Fjolnir was watching the illustration growing on the page. And then, as if he couldn't help himself, he said, "We were a lot further out than that."

"Were you?" I said mildly and turned to a fresh page to start again. "What could you see of the shore?"

"Runde," he said with a look of deep disdain on his face. "All the lights of Runde, such as they are."

"You don't have to be far out from shore to see that," I said even as I drew.

"We were not so far out as the shipping lanes for the cargo ships, because we can *never* go out that far," he said. As if that situation were terribly unfair somehow.

"Surely you don't need to, to catch fish?" I said.

"We went out further than we usually do, though," he said.

"Because the point of the thing wasn't to catch fish, was it?" I asked.

"I don't know," he said with a shrug. "I wasn't in charge."

"No, of course not," I said, and gave him an encouraging smile even as I continued adding rows of waves to the drawing.

"Mostly we catch herring, but sometimes I see other stuff," he said. He was talking low now, the sullen tone replaced by a conspiratorial sort of whisper.

"Rainbow smelt?" I asked as I drew.

"No, *other* stuff," he said.

I looked up from my drawing. He was speaking in earnest, not trying to mess with me.

"What other stuff?" I asked.

"I don't know," he said. "Sometimes I see other things moving through the water. But deep, deep down. And I see it more at night than by day."

"What's down there, do you think?" I asked.

"I don't know," he said. "But something is down there. Something big. Something I don't think I ever want to see."

"And yet, you keep looking for it," I said.

"I don't want to see it, but I don't want to miss seeing it either," he said. Then he shrugged.

"Did any of the others see what you saw?" I asked.

"I didn't see it last night," he said. "But I was looking."

"Okay," I said. "Has anyone else seen what you've seen when you've seen it?"

"No one *looks*," he said, crossing his arms tightly once more.

I looked down at my drawing, then back up at the boy. "I think we're done here. But I might want to talk to you again later, okay? After I've looked at some other things."

Like Fulla.

And maybe the lake itself.

"I guess," he said, but not with any particular enthusiasm.

"Roarr," I called, and he at once emerged from the shadows, Thormund and Esja close beside him.

"Ready to rejoin your family in the council hall?" Roarr asked a little too cheerfully.

Fjolnir just scowled at him. "I don't have a family. I live with my uncle. And he's out on patrol."

"Well, I know your aunt, Skefill's sister, is there. We'll have her watch out for you when we get there. And I know there's food and cider aplenty," I said.

"Did you learn anything new?" Esja asked me as I packed up my sketchbook and charcoal. Mjolner stood up on the bench and yawned massively. As if all the magical effort had been his.

"Not really," I sighed.

Because I already knew something lurked in the depths of that lake. I had even sensed it, back when I had been on a boat on those waters.

But I had been so young in my powers then. I knew I would sense so much more if I went out there again now.

Only I really didn't want to. I didn't want to know more about what lurked down there.

I really, truly didn't.

But to keep the people of Villmark safe, I was going to have to.

"Come on," I sighed, hefting my bag up onto my shoulder. "Let's go see how Fulla is doing."

With Fjolnir carefully positioned between Roarr and Thormund, our little party started south, down the main road to the council hall.

CHAPTER FOURTEEN

THE AIR that night was a little cooler than the last few nights, although the sky was still cloud-free. The moon was just beginning to wax once more, but so far was a mere sliver that illuminated little.

When we reached the massive front doors of the council hall, Thormund knocked with the butt of his spear. It was a loud knock in a complicated pattern, and we had to wait a moment after he was done before one of the doors opened, but only wide enough for us all to slip through one at a time.

I went first, followed by Esja. Despite the lack of light that shone around that door to the street outside, the interior of the hall was filled with cheery firelight from the immense braziers that ran in two rows down the sides of the audience chamber.

Some of the families were in the darker corners of the room, curled up on bedrolls with small children already fast asleep, unbothered by the strangeness of the last few days. Or too tired to fuss about it, perhaps.

Other families gathered close to that light, playing card and dice games to entertain the older children. Cider and cinnamon buns were everywhere, and I realized my grandmother had been much busier than I had thought. The cider I had known about, there were barrels of it that had been sent up over the last few weeks. But the buns she must have been baking herself. All day from dawn to dusk, before she opened the mead hall for business.

"There she is," Esja said, nudging me with her elbow.

I followed her jutting chin until I saw Fulla, sitting alone near one of the braziers. She had an open book spread across her lap, but wasn't even pretending to be reading it.

I turned to be sure that Fjolnir had come in with Roarr and Thormund behind me. He was there, hovering—sullenly, of course—as Thormund spoke to the two guards at the door.

Who, I realized, were Raggi and Skefill. They must have really chafed at this assignment. But their expressions now looked neither defiant nor particularly contrite. They were just carefully neutral as they listened and nodded to whatever Thormund was telling them.

Roarr took Fjolnir by the arm and led him over to the table where the cider barrels and plates stacked high with cinnamon buns were waiting. He saw me looking his way and gave me a little nod to tell me he would keep an eye on the boy.

I turned my attention back to Fulla, and Esja and I crossed the room to where she was sitting.

She looked up at me with red-rimmed, glassy eyes. Like she had cried out every tear she had in her and had no more outlet for her undiminished sorrow.

"Fulla," I said as I sank down at her side. Esja sat down on her other side, and even took one of her hands in both of hers.

"I guess you already know what happened," Fulla said dully.

"Esja and the Mikkelsens told me what they saw," I said. "Can you tell me what you saw?"

"Nothing," she said with a sniff. "I saw nothing at all. Brana's hand was in mine, and then it just slipped away. I turned around at once, I swear it. I think I was turning around before her fingers were even gone from mine. But she wasn't there. She was just gone."

"Did you feel anything odd?" I asked.

"Like cold or a wind or something?" Esja added when Fulla had brooded in silence for some time without answering my question.

"I don't think so," she said at last. "Just, Brana being gone. When her hand was gone from mine, that felt cold."

"Of course it did," Esja said, squeezing Fulla's hand all the tighter.

"Do you mind if I draw you?" I asked Fulla. "Sometimes that helps me figure things out."

"Of course, I know that," Fulla said. "Go ahead."

I chose pencils this time, and she rested her hands on the open pages of her book, sitting with her back perfectly straight. She would make a lovely model for figure drawing, just the normal artistic variety.

But when I was done, although I had a lovely portrait of a very sad girl trying so hard to keep a brave face on, I saw nothing in the details of the sketch that gave me any clues.

Not even any lake imagery.

Although I kind of wondered if that was because my fears had been riled up a bit by Fjolnir's words. I might be too cautious about it to be open to the sensations now.

I sighed. Perhaps too loudly, as Fulla quickly asked, "What is it? Did I do something wrong?"

"No, it's me," I said. Then I summoned up a smile. "Don't worry about it. I'm going to figure this out."

"I know you are," Fulla said. "You always do."

Well, I always had before. That didn't mean I always would.

But there was no way I was going to express that thought out loud.

I just smiled at her again.

But something going on across the room caught my attention. There was a commotion near the doors, although it was clearly a commotion that those involved were trying to keep on the down low.

Still, I looked over at Esja and saw that she had noticed it, too.

"Get some rest," I told Fulla. Then Esja and I went back across the hall to the shadowy area near the doors.

Raggi and Skefill were speaking urgently to Roarr, but their whispers were too low for me to catch a single word. Esja and I reached their side just as Thormund returned from something he had been doing outside.

"What is it?" I asked, keeping my own voice low.

"It's Fjolnir," Skefill said. He looked pale, although in the shadows, it was a little hard to be sure.

"He's missing," Roarr told me.

"Not outside," Thormund added.

"He was taken?" I asked.

I hated that thought. A lot. It meant a couple of changes to the modus operandi of whatever was hunting us.

This would be the first male victim, for one.

The first taken from indoors, for two.

And if he was truly taken from inside the hall, which was filled with people, none of whom had seen a thing?

That thought really chilled me to my very soul.

"I think he just slipped away," Thormund said to me. So I guess my terror had been a little too apparent on my face. I tried to school my features into something more neutral and less likely to alarm the others.

"We were right here the entire time," Raggi said.

"I swear, Ingrid Torfudottir, we did not knowingly let him out," Skefill said. He even placed a fist over his heart so that I knew he was swearing a true vow.

"I know," I said. I knew the horror he had felt when he realized he might have inadvertently put his cousins in danger hadn't been faked. And nothing that had happened since had done anything but reinforce the role of the lake.

He had been watching me draw, at least for the first seven of the fishermen. He knew everything had been about the lake. The depths of that lake.

"We should check the boats first," Roarr said to me.

"Let's go," I said, with a nod to Thormund.

But after returning my nod, Thormund spun to catch Raggi and Skefill each by an arm and hiss at them both, "You are both in charge here. Swear you won't make me regret that choice."

"We won't," Raggi said, lifting his chin in answer to the challenge.

"As much as we can, we shall do," Skefill said. I could see the possible fate of Fjolnir was already weighing on him.

"He's probably down by the boats," I said to him. "We'll catch him before he can find real trouble."

"I know you will try," was all Skefill managed to say in response.

I wanted to give him a supportive hug, but I didn't think he'd take that well. So I just gestured for Raggi to open the door. Once again, he only pulled it open the minimum amount for me to slip out into the night beyond.

Roarr followed close at my heels, but Esja lingered to give Skefill that hug I hadn't had the nerve to try for. He stood in stiff shock at first, but then melted a bit as her arms refused to let him go until he returned the gesture.

"We'll find him," she said to him. And then she was outside with Roarr and me.

Thormund came through last, and the door boomed shut behind him with a finality that made that shiver run up my spine again.

"The Mikkelsens are down by the boats," Thormund told us even as he led the way at a jog north to the village square.

"I doubt he is going to steal a boat with those two on guard," Roarr said.

I hoped he was right. And I managed to hold on to that hope all the way to the meadow overlooking the ridge, and down through the caves to the largest cavern of all.

This was the harbor for all the Villmarker ships. They lay hidden behind the shimmering curtain of the waterfall, their presence unknown to the world of Runde beyond.

The fishermen would sneak through a side channel, passing down the river to the lake beyond with only the residual magic from the barrier my ancestor Torfa had erected to protect them from notice. And so far, that had always been enough.

But the vessel that dominated the harbor was the longship, and that one was too large to ever not be noticed. Not without a volva on board.

We hadn't taken it out this year. Even though it had always been a yearly tradition. We had taken it out the year before, but my mormor had been aboard that time, supervising my efforts to weave the spells that kept the longship safe.

No one this year had even asked. And I hadn't realized.

Was my aversion to the lake so obvious to the others?

Or was this a sign that they still didn't trust me? Not the way they trusted my grandmother.

I was still ruminating about all those currently irrelevant things when Nilda called out, "Who goes there?" in her deepest, most commanding voice.

"It's fine," Kara said from directly behind me, and I turned to see her with both of her swords out in her hands. "It's just Ingrid and company."

"Ingrid," Nilda said as she emerged from the shadows by the shed that stood where the dock met the shore. "What are you doing down here?"

"No one else has been here?" I asked almost breathlessly.

"Just you," Kara said.

"Count the boats," Thormund said, even as he ran down the length of the dock to do just that.

"What's going on?" Nilda asked.

"Skefill's cousin Fjolnir might have sneaked down here to steal a boat," I said.

Although that didn't sound right, even as I said it. He was as unnerved by whatever hid under the lake as I was.

Only, what was it he had said? The only thing worse than seeing it was not seeing it? I hadn't been paying a lot of attention at the time, but I knew what he meant now.

Whatever was under the lake, it wasn't something that it was safe to take your eyes off of. It was like being in a room with an angry, venomous snake. You wanted to know where that snake was the entire time.

"We're missing a kayak," Thormund said from where he was standing, no longer on the dock but on the far side of that shed. There was a rack there that held stacked canoes and kayaks. It was pretty haphazard stacking. I'm not sure how he knew just one was missing, and that it was a kayak.

And yet, I didn't doubt him for a minute.

"There's no way," Nilda said, gaping at her sister.

"If it's connected to what's happening in town, there absolutely is a way," I said. "He got out of a hall full of people, past a door guarded by two men. A door so heavy it's impossible to quietly open it without being noticed."

"This isn't your fault," Roarr added, in case my meaning wasn't clear.

"What now?" Kara asked as she put her swords away.

She and her sister and Esja and Roarr shifted their attention back and forth between me and Thormund. Then Thormund too looked at me with a helpless sort of shrug.

What could we do?

But I knew. There was only one answer.

"We take the longship out," I said.

CHAPTER FIFTEEN

I HAD DONE THIS BEFORE. Sure, it had been months ago, but I had learned so much in the months since then. I knew far more about the barrier that protected Villmark, and about the layers upon layers of spells that protected my grandmother's mead hall in Runde.

I could do this.

So why was I so nervous?

Thormund insisted that he and Roarr, with the help of Esja and the Mikkelsen sisters, would be enough to navigate the longship on such a still, almost moonless night. He was at the rudder, ready to guide the ship down the curves of the river until we reached the lake. Roarr and Esja sat at two of the oars on the port side, and Nilda and Kara did the same on the starboard side. We weren't going to go fast, at least not until we reached the lake and I could summon a wind to fill the sails, but that was all right. The current of the river would keep us moving more than the efforts of the rowers.

No, the weak link in this whole plan was definitely my apprehension about going back out onto that lake.

But Fjolnir was either our culprit, or he was a particularly tragic victim being led to some bad fate. Either way, we had to get to him before he got to wherever he was kayaking to.

So I took my seat on the three-legged stool just fore of Thormund's position at the rudder. It was a sturdy piece of furniture, the three legs thick and splayed wide. It would take quite a wave to topple me over while I was sitting there.

I sat on the stool with my art bag between my feet and closed my eyes, just feeling the sense of the barrier flickering before me. No one else could see it, and even I didn't so much see it as just feel it there, between the dragon-shaped prow of the ship and the glowing curtain of the waterfall by starlight.

Then I raised my hands and gestured for those waters to part. Everyone saw that, and took it as a signal to start rowing, to bring the ship out of the calm of its subterranean harbor and out into the flow of the river.

What they didn't see was that, as well as parting the water, my hands had parted that magical barrier. We brought a shimmer of it with us as we passed through it, enough to help me keep that ship unnoticed from the eyes of ordinary northern Minnesotans.

No theme park ride could ever match the feeling of slipping through that parted waterfall. I could feel the chill of its spray on my face, and the sound of it crashing onto the rocks was a continuous roar. But only when we'd reached the far side did the curtain fall closed again behind us, a proper waterfall once more.

Esja was the only one rowing who had never done this before. She had never even been on the longship before. But Roarr was whispering instructions to her to keep their strokes matched with the Mikkelsens' on the other side. Which they had to do; the river current directly under the waterfall was almost a whirlpool, and the ship very much wanted to spin in place rather than follow the path of the water out to the lake. Especially this night, when it was so very lightly weighted down. We were practically bobbing on the surface of the water.

Then Thormund at the rudder caught the flow, and we were zipping along silently, past the rocky shore where the path up to Villmark hid on our left, and past the expanse of Swanson family farms on our right.

My hands were in constant motion, weaving the protection spells, although it felt like we scarcely needed them, the night was so dark and the ship so noiseless over the water. Still, it was an effort. It was harder to ground the spells around the ever-moving ship than it was in my grandmother's mead hall. They kept trying to slip away, to trail behind the ship over the water where they'd do us no good at all.

But I had it under control.

And once we reached the mouth of the river and had slipped out over the surface of the lake itself, Thormund called for Roarr to deploy the single sail.

It was a bit of an effort for about ten minutes, as I struggled to both maintain the cloaking magic while also drawing wavy lines in the air with my bronze wand to summon breezes to fill that sail. But the breezes complied readily, and we had soon sped far enough out over the water that we were no longer clearly visible from shore.

I let the cloaking spells drop just a little. We had to keep an eye out for boats and ships around us. If any came near, I'd have to bring those spells back up.

But for a moment, anyway, I could relax a little. The wind, once summoned, liked to hang around, so that was no work for me now.

But there was still the matter of finding a seventeen-year-old boy in dark clothes paddling a kayak with no reflective strips or anything to help us find him in the dark.

Where would he have gone?

"A kayak," Kara said musingly. "Do you suppose that means he intends to stay close to shore? Maybe he's going up another inlet somewhere. There are so many creeks that empty into the lake along this coast."

"I think he stole the kayak because that was all he *could* steal," Thormund said. "Not with you two on guard duty."

"We failed," Nilda pointed out.

"He wouldn't have been able to handle any of the boats on his own, anyway," Roarr said. "No, he took the kayak because he had to. And I had specifically warned you to watch out for a gang of men looking to launch a boat, not just one boy."

Nilda said nothing, but I could see she was still kicking herself over not noticing him there. I resisted the urge to explain about the magic again.

Mostly because I still didn't understand it. Was the magic manipulating him, drawing him out here? Or was he manipulating the magic, using it to get where he wanted to go?

I still didn't know.

But I pulled my sketchbook out of my bag and turned to the page I had drawn while chatting with him just a few hours before. There were no clues in the drawing, I knew that already.

But that didn't mean it wasn't still useful.

I drew my bronze wand and danced it in the air in front of me while I pictured everything I had been channeling when I had drawn that picture. I hadn't exactly been in a fugue state, not like I'd been with the first seven fishermen. But I had been in a more magically receptive state. Call it fugue-adjacent.

I had been drinking in an essence that was uniquely Fjolnir.

I just hoped I could use it now to find him. Somewhere.

There was a lot of water around us. A lot of steel gray water.

And ever so much more below us.

"Ingrid?" Esja called softly.

"I'm searching for him," I told her as my wand continued its dance. If anything, I was sure to the rest of them it just looked like I was conducting an imaginary orchestra.

But I wasn't. I was sensing magic. Both the essence of the boy who had told me about his fears of this water, but also the remnants of the barrier spells. We all carried fragments of that magic on us from our journey through the waterfall.

Fjolnir would have even more. Because he hadn't parted that barrier. He had just powered through it. He'd be coated with it.

"Further out, I'm afraid," I said when I finally had to admit that I was sensing a clear direction, even if it was the direction I least wanted to go.

"Northeast or due east?" Thormund asked, both hands on the rudder.

"That way," I said, stabbing with my wand. Because I hadn't brought a compass with me, and while I had little doubt that Thormund could read the stars, I still could not.

The others waited on their benches, oars held high out of the water but at the ready should they be needed. But the sail snapped twice before catching the stiff breeze once more, and the ship danced over the low swells, zipping us ever further from home.

I had gone out further than this before, with a full complement of crew. In broad daylight. With both my grandmother and Thorbjorn there with me.

But now I was in the dark. And neither of them were with me.

So I suppose it was no wonder that my heart beat so hard as we left the last glimpse of that tree- and rock-covered shoreline behind. It felt so very isolating, having nothing around you but black sky and gray water.

I could only imagine how much worse this journey must be for Fjolnir, alone in a kayak. If anything should go wrong, if he should get dumped into the lake for whatever reason, even in the height of summer, that was a recipe for hypothermia.

And this mid-September night was very far from the height of summer. He'd freeze in minutes. And, being alone, there would be no one there to help him.

That, that would be so very isolating. Just the fear of it must be mind-numbing. How did he keep rowing?

And yet, clearly, he was. Because there was still no sign of him up ahead of us. I knew he was there, in that direction, somewhere. But I didn't know how far ahead he was.

I could only hope we would find him soon.

CHAPTER SIXTEEN

IT WAS LONG past midnight but nowhere near dawn when Esja started making little complaining noises. Like she was in discomfort, but was trying not to whine out loud.

"Are you all right?" Roarr asked her, his voice pitched low but not quite a whisper. "This is your first time out. The water is pretty calm, but maybe you're getting boat sick?"

"No, I'm not nauseous," Esja said. "It's not a headache either. I just feel... wrong."

"Wrong how?" Kara asked.

But I had already taken all my attention away from the search for Fjolnir and his kayak to wave my wand between my eyes and where Esja was huddling on her bench, hugging herself as if she were cold.

There was definitely something going on with her. I could see a glow to her that shouldn't be there. But I couldn't see where it was coming from, unless she was generating it herself.

"Ingrid," Roarr said.

And just from the way he said my name, I knew he was seeing what he had seen with Esja before. What he called the un-thing. It was taking over her.

Then Esja's whole body went rigid and her eyes rolled back until just the whites were visible. Although those whites were far too intense for the little light that was illuminating us on the boat.

It was like something was lighting her up from within.

I heard Thormund behind me swear softly, but he never left the rudder.

Nilda and Kara started to lunge across the boat to reach Esja's sides, but Roarr gestured for them to stay back.

"Esja?" he called softly.

Esja's blank eyes turned his way, and she started to speak. But the words she used were completely foreign to me.

The last time I had heard her speak in such a state, I had been able to piece together what she was saying. It had been a very old variant of the old Norse that had become Villmarker Norse over time, and I could just barely understand it.

But this? This was like nothing I had ever heard.

And, to judge from the confused looks on everyone else's faces, like nothing any of them had ever heard before either.

"Esja," I said in my most commanding voice.

Esja said something that sounded negatory, like she was denying that was her name. It sent chills up my spine, the way her voice grated sounds out. As if her vocal cords had turned to stone.

"Why is this starting now?" Roarr asked.

Which was a very good question.

I got up from my stool and scanned the horizon. But it didn't take long to find what I was looking for.

Directly ahead of us, not so far away as the horizon and hence difficult to see over the dark waters, I just discerned what I was sure was the shadow of Fjolnir in his kayak.

But even as I pointed it out to the others, the water by that kayak started to churn.

And Esja's strange voice grew louder and her chanting faster as if in response to that change.

"Ingrid?" Kara said nervously.

But before I could summon any words at all, the churning of the water became a splashing wave as something immense thrust up out from the deep, breaking the surface to launch up into the air. It blotted the lights from the stars beyond it, but all I could make out was a vague sense of an outline.

It was like what little light there was just didn't want to touch whatever it was that had just risen up out of the water. The light darted away from it, leaving a patch of darkest shadow that my eyes couldn't penetrate.

But then Esja stopped chanting to say a word that we all knew well.

"Nidhogg."

Nidhogg, the dragon from the old stories that lurks deep underground in the realm of Niflheim. From there, it gnaws at the roots of the World Tree Yggdrasil. The damage it does is mended by the Norns using the waters from their well, but it is always a mere delaying of the inevitable end.

That end being Nidhogg chewing all the way through the roots of Yggdrasil that kept it bound and escaping from Niflheim.

Needless to say, that's not supposed to happen until Ragnarok.

Which I really hoped wasn't today.

"No," I said. My effort to sound calm and confident were a bit undercut when I had to swallow hard before getting any more words out. "No, this is something else."

"Are you sure?" Kara asked, alternating between peering into that shadow and glancing nervously over at Esja.

Who had resumed her creepy chanting.

"It has to be," I said. "Niflheim isn't under this lake. But something is."

"Fjolnir is still out there," Nilda said. "But I can't see what's going on."

"No, that's magical darkness for sure," I said.

Luckily, making light had been one of the first things I had learned how to do with magic. It was also one of the easiest.

It was almost like the entire world preferred the light to the darkness.

I summoned a ball of magical light, then used my wand to throw that ball far out over the water.

I was never particularly good at any of the ball sports, or aiming in general, but the magical light didn't need my efforts to home in on where I wanted it to go. It was like it was attracted to that unnatural darkness.

It reached the boundary of the shadow and stopped as if trapped in a sticky membrane. But then it burst through again, stopping at a point just over the dragon's nose.

Because it was definitely a dragon. And it was a lot larger than I had thought. Only its head and neck were visible against the background of the starry sky. From the shoulders down, the rest of its body was underwater.

But that neck, that long, toothy maw, were both large enough to swallow our longship, mast and all, in one mighty gulp.

And Fjolnir, in his little kayak, bobbed in the water before it. He had thrown back the hood of his cloak, and I could see the light from my magic sphere dancing over his dampened locks of hair.

The look on his face was one of blank bliss. Even when the dragon bent its neck to put the tip of its snout closer to him.

We were too far away to see clearly, even with the addition of the bright light, but I was sure I saw something happen. The dragon opened its massive jaws and unfurled its serpent-like tongue. The tip of that tongue snapped in the air like a whip, then—as if that snapping had been the stretch before a focused exercise—it probed gently towards Fjolnir's face.

Fjolnir opened his mouth wide, as wide as it would go. And the tip of the dragon's tongue met his with a flash of light.

I was sure I had seen all of that, despite the distance.

I just wasn't sure what any of it meant.

But Esja's chanting was growing loud and urgent once more. If it had been just her and me on that boat, I would've realized what she was about to do too late to stop her.

But it wasn't just the two of us. And Roarr was not only much closer to her than I was, but was also paying much closer attention to what she was doing. The instant she lunged for the side of the ship to throw herself over, he was already jumping to tackle her.

He caught her tightly in his arms, then rolled with her trapped against his chest until they were lying in the middle of the boat. She struggled, strong enough to nearly buck him off several times despite the fact he easily had six inches and more than fifty pounds on her.

"There it goes," Nilda said, and I looked away from Esja and Roarr to see the dragon sliding back down beneath the waves.

The lake returned to its almost calm state far too quickly. There was no sign anything had ever been there at all, except that my light glowed still.

But it lit nothing but water. Fjolnir in his kayak had already disappeared into the darkness once more.

"What do we do?" Kara asked. "Do we go after the boy or after the dragon?"

"How can we possibly go after the dragon?" Thormund said. "Do you have any idea how deep the lake is here?"

"No," Kara said. "Do you?"

"It's about two hundred meters down from here," Thormund said. "Not the deepest point in the lake. That would be further east than we generally go. But deep."

"Oh," Kara said, and sat back down on her bench.

I kind of felt the same way. If you'd asked me ten minutes before if I thought Thormund even knew what a meter was, I don't think I would've guessed the answer was yes.

But two hundred meters was definitely deeper than we could ever hope to go. I didn't think even SCUBA divers could go down that deep. Not without space age technology like breathing liquid oxygen or something.

We'd need a submersible. Which I doubted we'd ever have access to.

My magic definitely wasn't going to cut it.

"I don't see Fjolnir at all," Nilda said from where she had positioned herself at the prow. She was leaning half out over the water, staring intently all around where my magic sphere still hovered, its light dancing in silver sparkles over the water.

Esja was still making noises of protest in that language none of us could understand. But Roarr was making no move to let her up yet, even though her struggles had lost all their strength.

"Ingrid?" Thormund said from behind me.

I chewed at my lip as I mulled it all over.

I wanted more than anything to confront that dragon. It *had* to be the thing I kept sensing in the lake, the lurking menace that had been haunting me for nearly a year now. I had finally put a face to it, even if the name "Nidhogg" still didn't feel quite right.

But I didn't have what I needed for that confrontation now. I lacked the volva ability *still*, I was sure.

I lacked a way to safely get down to the bottom of the lake and back up again after.

I lacked the aid of Loke and Thorbjorn.

It simply wasn't time.

And I *hated* it. I wanted it to be the time. I wanted to face this fight and get it over with.

But I couldn't.

I didn't realize I had started laughing bitterly out loud until everyone turned to stare at me in alarm.

"Sorry," I said. "I just figured out what naudhr really means."

"Which is?" Kara asked, her eyebrows raised high. Like she still thought she might be talking to a crazy person.

"I have to work with my destiny, not fight against it," I said. "And while this will almost certainly be where I end up eventually, it's not where I'm meant to be now."

"So we're going after the boy?" Nilda asked.

I raised my wand and extinguished the magic light with a flick of my wrist. "No," I said as I tucked the wand away again. "But only because we don't need to go *after* him. We know where he's going, and we can get there faster than he can."

"Back to Villmark?" Thormund said, already leaning on the rudder.

"Back to Villmark," I said, and shifted my concentration enough to get the magical breezes filling our sail again.

"And what about Esja?" Roarr asked.

I walked fore until I was standing just behind him, looking over his shoulder at Esja pinned beneath him. She was lying motionless now, save for shivers that wracked her body in waves.

Then she blinked and looked up at me with her normal blue eyes.

"I think you can let her up," I said, resting a hand on his shoulder for just a moment. "But stay close to her. I think it was the dragon and not Fjolnir she was reacting to, but something passed from that dragon to him." Or possibly the other way around, although that idea disturbed me so greatly, I was loath to voice it. "Best not to take any chances."

"Here," Nilda said as she approached with a warm woolen blanket in her hands. She had gotten it from the chest in the front of the ship, I guessed. Roarr helped Esja sit up, and Nilda wrapped first the blanket and then her own arms around Esja's shaking body.

"It's over?" Esja said to me.

"For now," I said.

Although even that much, I was only guessing at.

There was still so much of the night left to go.

CHAPTER SEVENTEEN

THE EFFORT TO keep the breezes filling the sail had felt minimal before. But by the time the shore was in view, I could feel an absolutely wicked headache forming behind my eyes.

Maybe it was just that I had never done much sustained magic before. Even contributing to the ever-present spells over the mead hall was just about getting them going and then leaving them to continue doing their own thing.

This was a continuous effort.

I had never run a marathon, but I was sure what I was experiencing now was like a first-time runner realizing several miles in that how good it felt in the first five minutes was no indication as to how the rest of it was going to go.

In short, I was exhausted.

And Esja was still looking peaky. She hadn't said anything that wasn't in modern Villmarker Norse the entire trip home, and then only the fewest, most necessary words. And she hadn't tried to throw herself overboard. Neither had her eyes gone all white again.

But she looked worse than I felt, and that was saying something.

"Nearly there," Kara said. "Let me flow some magic into you before you slide us past Runde, okay?"

"Yes, thank you," I said, grateful that she had volunteered. I hadn't even thought of asking for her help.

The flow of her magic into me was soft and gentle, more emotionally reassuring than actually magically useful to me. But I had needed that reassurance so badly.

"We split up from here," Thormund said as the Mikkelsens jumped down to the dock to make the ship fast. "Roarr and I will find Fjolnir. Nilda and Kara, get Ingrid and Esja safely home. They're both clearly done for the night."

Esja and I both started weakly protesting at once. Thormund didn't argue back. He just carried on as if he couldn't even hear us.

"Let them catch Fjolnir," Nilda said to me as she and Kara both held out their hands to help me down from the ship. Usually I tried to do that on my own, but this time I accepted their help without a word.

"I think you should focus on what just happened to Esja," Kara said. "We'll go back to your house, and maybe you can draw or something?"

"Sure," I said, patting the art bag at my side wearily. "I can draw."

Esja said nothing. She still had the blanket from the ship around her shoulders as we trudged up out of the caves, then across the meadow and through Villmark.

We passed a single patrol who greeted us without stopping. Then we crossed the village commons and turned south to the front gate of my house.

Mjolner was sitting on the fence post by the gate as if he was waiting for us. But when we went inside the house, he made no move to follow us. I was tempted to leave the door open for him, but that was silly.

Mjolner could walk through walls. Why would I need to leave a door open for him?

I really must be tired.

And yet, sleep wasn't in my future. Even as Nilda and Kara helped Esja get cleaned up, undressed, and into bed, all I could do was fix a pot of coffee so strong even Roarr would have to admire it and consume a big mug of it before heading back upstairs.

"She fell asleep the minute her head hit the pillow," Kara whispered to me as I stood in the doorway, sketchbook and pencil already in hand.

"Where do you want us?" Nilda asked.

"Downstairs should be fine," I said. "Maybe stand near the front door so you can keep an ear out. Just in case any of the patrols finds something or there's an alarm or something."

"Sure," Nilda said.

We passed in the doorway as the two of them tiptoed out and down the stairs. I slipped into the chair beside Esja's bed.

She was indeed deeply asleep. But it didn't seem like a restful sleep. She stirred a lot, sort of mumbling to herself. I couldn't hear what she was saying, but it didn't sound like the words she had spoken back on the ship. At least, it definitely wasn't that voice like grating stones.

I sat back in the chair. This chair was something Esja had acquired after moving in. It was puffy, almost over-stuffed, and looked like striped candy, all pearly white and soft pink. She liked to curl up in it sideways with a book, and with the well-padded arms, it was almost like it had been built to be used that way.

But I sat in the conventional way, if with one foot up to rest my heel on the seat so I could keep my sketchbook at an upward angle as I drew.

First, I just drew Esja, as she was sleeping there. Then I turned the page and drew her again, this time as I remembered her from that first moment on the ship when she had looked at me with her white eyes and started to speak.

I turned another page and scribbled on, my drawings getting sketchier as the images flowed through me faster and faster. Esja trying to get into the water. Not to get to the dragon, as I had half-thought at the time, but to flee away from it.

Then I drew the dragon itself, all long flowing lines that became mere suggestions of shadows below the waterline.

If my drawing were true, the size of that entire dragon was immense. Like a dinosaur.

But before I had quite processed what I was drawing, I was turning another page and drawing again.

This time the image spilling out of the tip of my pencil was of an anonymous street in Villmark. My hand gripping the pencil seemed to know precisely what it was drawing, but I couldn't say I recognized any of the houses taking shape on the page.

I didn't get much of an opportunity to look, though, before I was turning the page again and drawing another scene. A head barely visible in a row of shrubberies. Whoever the head belonged to was peering in an unshuttered window. Watching a woman alone in a kitchen fussing with a kettle over an open fire.

I didn't recognize the woman, but I was pretty sure the head belonged to Fjolnir. It looked like his tousled locks, anyway.

Another rapid turning of a page, and another scene emerging on the blank paper. It was more clearly Fjolnir now, as he crept up to the kitchen door of that house. The window was no longer in view, but somehow I knew that woman was still in there. Still making herself a late night cup of tea.

Still unaware that danger lurked right outside her door.

"Nilda," I called, or tried to. My voice came out choked and weak, but I couldn't seem to focus on it properly to try again.

I was drawing yet another scene. Fjolnir, his hand on the knob of that door now.

If he was the one who had been abducting people all along, this was a horrifying escalation. He was about to snatch a woman out of her own kitchen?

And yet, if he wasn't our culprit, what *was* he doing?

"Ingrid?" Nilda said softly from the doorway. Like she wasn't sure if I had called out to her or not. Like if I hadn't, she didn't want to interrupt me.

But I couldn't focus enough to answer her. All my attention was on the sound of Esja's restless breathing, and the images flowing out of my pencil.

A new scene. Fjolnir, still at that kitchen door. But he wasn't touching the knob anymore. No, he had been tackled to the ground.

The sketch was a chaos of emotive lines, but I was pretty sure the blurring forms that were on top of him were Thormund and Roarr both.

I vaguely heard Nilda and Kara whispering together, both in the doorway now, as I turned to the very last page in my sketchbook and drew in another hasty scrawl.

Fjolnir, his mouth open wide. At first I thought this was a reaction to getting the breath knocked out of him after getting tackled by two large, full-grown men.

But then I saw it was the glowing thing, like a disk of light. The thing that the dragon's tongue had placed inside his mouth.

Or the thing that had been there all along, but had glowed at the dragon's touch.

Either way, it was coming out now.

And it was going to get away.

"No!" I cried, jumping from the chair and sending my sketchbook flying.

"What is it?" Nilda asked, but I just pushed past her, running down the stairs to get to where I had left my art bag near my easel. I pulled out my wand, then ran outside into the street.

The kitchen I had drawn. The woman inside of it. She had been making tea with a kettle over an open fire. That wasn't a great clue, but the more traditional homes in Villmark tended to be on the western side of town, so I ran that way first.

Then I saw Mjolner, running ahead of me. Like he was leading the way. I followed him, west and then north and then west again.

We found the house in question without ever slowing our sprint. And Thormund and Roarr were still there, helping a limp Fjolnir to his feet.

The woman stood in her kitchen doorway, her hands clasped together over her chest in alarm.

But where was the ball of light?

Mjolner meowed loudly and launched up into the sky like he sometimes did when he was messing with birds in my grandmother's garden.

But he didn't catch it. And I didn't realize what he was batting at until it was past me, too.

That ball of light blasted past me with all the crazy speed and absolute silence of a UFO.

I turned to follow it, but there was no sign which way it had gone.

Although I could guess. Back to the lake. Back to that dragon lurking under the lake.

And it had gone at such a speed, there was no use in my trying to follow after it.

I turned back to Thormund and Roarr.

"I saw it," Roarr told me, as if I looked like I needed a little confirmation that I wasn't crazy. "It's gone now, though. And all the extreme strength Fjolnir was fighting us with left with it."

"Fjolnir?" Thormund said to the boy.

Fjolnir was breathing hard, sucking in air in irregular jerks. It took me a minute to figure out he was trying hard not to cry.

"Are you hurt?" I asked. Just from what I'd seen in my pencil sketch, it looked like Thormund and Roarr had hit him pretty hard.

But he just shook his head even as he continued fighting to get his breath back.

I was pretty sure he was back in his own head, though. His lanky adolescent posture had returned, shoulders hunched and head dipped low so that his hair covered his face and eyes.

Even so, he needed to be watched. And more closely than we'd been watching him before.

The night still was far from over.

CHAPTER EIGHTEEN

I LED the way back to my house, Mjolner trotting along at my heels, Thormund and Roarr following behind with a limp Fjolnir supported between them.

My house was closer than the council hall. But it was also far more secure. The last thing I wanted to do was bring Fjolnir back to the safe haven where all the young families were. Better he was in my own home, if he still had it in him to make any trouble.

Not that he looked like he did. He was half-asleep even as we reached my front door.

"What do you want to do with him?" Thormund asked.

"Let's just put him in my bed for now," Roarr said before I could answer. "Poor kid. He's had a long night."

"We've all had a long night," Thormund grumbled.

But at my nod, the two of them brought Fjolnir upstairs.

And I went into my kitchen to make another pot of that extra-strength coffee, as Nilda and Kara had consumed the last of the pot while I was away.

After it had brewed, I brought a tray of mugs up the stairs. Two for Thormund and Roarr, watching over Fjolnir as he slept as quiet as a corpse on top of Roarr's covers, and two more for Nilda and Kara.

They were watching over Esja, and I was relieved to see that Esja was sleeping more naturally now. Her ragged breathing was smooth, and the tension lines were gone from her face on the pillow.

I picked up my sketchbook from where it had fallen and took it to my own bedroom. Not that I thought I was going to get any sleep. I just wanted a few quiet moments alone to look it over in the light of my bedside lamp.

Mjolner hopped up onto the bed beside me, curling up on half of the pillow as if this were a perfectly normal bedtime at the end of a perfectly normal day.

I just sat with my back against the headboard, vaguely aware of the sky to the east brightening as I turned through the pages of my sketchbook.

I was searching the backgrounds for clues. Some hint of runes I had drawn unconsciously that might tell me more than the main images in the illustrations themselves.

But I found nothing. I even went back to the first pages, to all the drawings of the lake I had done while talking with Skefill's cousins. But while the impression of something in the deep was stronger now that I knew it was literally true, I saw nothing new.

I sighed and closed the book just as the first rays of the rising sun reached over the ridge to the east and shone straight through my bedroom window, lighting the whole room up in a golden glow that was its own kind of magic.

But I only had a moment to enjoy that quiet peace before yet another morning was marred by a loud pounding on my front door.

I hopped up despite Mjolner's sleepy yowl of protest, then ran out of my room.

"I've got it," I said to Nilda in Esja's doorway. Then I said it again as Thormund peered out of Roarr's room.

I took the stairs two at a time, then jogged down the long down-stairs hallway to my front door.

And threw it open just as Skefill's fist was coming down to knock again. He retracted it just in time to avoid knocking on my face.

He looked as exhausted as I felt. And Raggi behind him looked no better.

Skefill lowered his hand with an embarrassed grimace. But he quickly schooled his features back to a stern glare. "My cousin is here?"

"Yes, he's here," I said. "I'm not sure I want to let you see him, though."

"You think you could stop us?" Raggi asked in a challenge, but Skefill raised a hand to silence him.

"Is he all right?" Skefill asked me earnestly.

"I don't know," I said. "I really don't."

Then I gave him and Raggi a brief account of everything that had happened that night. I watched the emotions shift over their faces as I described the stolen kayak, then the dragon far out over the lake.

Then Fjolnir attempting to sneak into a woman's kitchen for clearly nefarious purposes.

And I took a little heart from what I saw. Because they were clearly surprised by all of it.

And they weren't doubting me.

Those were both important details.

"Ingrid," Roarr called softly from the stairs. I turned to see him leaning over the railing just enough to be seen from the front door. "Fjolnir is awake."

"I'll be right there," I said.

Then I turned back to Raggi and Skefill. "I'm going to trust the two of you. Because I need to. The whole town needs all of us to trust each other and work together. Do you understand that?"

"We've been doing all we can," Raggi said.

"Well," Skefill said with a flush to his cheeks. "We could've done better."

"We could've been allowed into the decision-making process more," Raggi shot back. "Taking orders is fine. But I want to be there when those orders are decided on. And having a voice in that decision would be better."

And actually, I had no argument against that. In fact, it seemed like just the thing to bring the isolationists more inside the fold.

They had kept themselves apart from the council on purpose, I knew. In the early days of their movement, they had listened a little too much to the old man known as Odd. Odd had been a trouble-maker, a trickster, a bad influence of the first order.

But Odd had died months ago. And without his constant strife-creating influence, even the staunchest isolationist might be persuaded to at least listen.

And if these two wanted to go beyond listening to actively partici-pating? I was all in.

It would mean hearing more of their rhetoric. And if their will was thwarted by the council too much, I knew they'd take it badly.

But that was a problem for another day. If it ever came up at all.

"I will get that for you," I promised them both. "I will speak to the council, and especially to Valki, who is the chief one in charge of the patrols and things you'd want to be part of. You will have a voice, I promise you."

"And in return?" Raggi asked, crossing his arms and glaring down at me.

Even though I was standing a step higher than they were. That was annoying.

But I just lifted my chin and said, "I'm going to need you to help me keep Fjolnir safe."

"You scarcely needed to bargain for that," Skefill said with real relief. What did he think I was going to ask of them?

"Well, we'll see how you feel when I give you all the details," I said. "But first, let's go see how Fjolnir is doing."

I waited for the two of them to pry off their boots in my mudroom, then led the way up the stairs to Roarr's bedroom door, right at the top of the staircase.

Fjolnir was sitting up on Roarr's bed, scratching at the back of his head and yawning widely.

"He claims not to remember a thing," Thormund told me with deep skepticism.

"Let's see," I said, and sat down at the edge of the foot of the bed. Fjolnir looked like he was uncomfortable having me so close, but after a glance traded with his cousin in the doorway, he opted to say nothing.

"How are you feeling?" I asked him first.

"Like I got crushed under a boulder," he said, rubbing at his ribs. "I think I've got bruises even."

I said nothing, just studied his face and especially his eyes. But he seemed perfectly honest. He didn't remember getting tackled by Thormund and Roarr at all. He was genuinely confused by the soreness of his body. Although I was sure he had competed in enough violent sports in his day to know what being tackled by bigger bodies felt like.

"What's the last thing you remember?" I asked, even as he blinked, looking around the room and realizing he didn't know where he was.

"I was in the council hall with the others," he said. "Where am I now?"

But I ignored that question. "Be more specific. What is the last thing you remember happening inside that hall? I'll get you started. We all came inside. Esja and I went to talk to Fulla, and you were near Thormund and Roarr as they spoke to your cousin and Raggi by the door."

"Right," he said slowly. He had stopped looking around, but he was still absent-mindedly rubbing his own ribs. "That was after we talked about the lake."

"Quite a bit after," I said. "We did that up on the commons."

"Yeah, right," he said. But I could tell he was only playing along. His memories were more jumbled than I had guessed.

"I was still thinking about the lake," he said at last, but softly. Like he was afraid something outside the room might overhear him. "I was remembering what it was like looking into the lake." He took a shaky breath and dipped his chin low, so that his hair fell over his eyes again. Like he needed that veiling. "I was in the hall, but I was thinking about the lake. Then it was like the hall wasn't even there around me anymore. It was just the lake. And I was falling into it. I know that sounds stupid."

"It's not stupid," I said.

"No, it is, though," he said almost venomously. "I mean, yeah, you can fall into a lake. But once you're in it, you're sinking, right? Only I wasn't. I was *in* the lake, but I was falling. Just falling and falling. And then I was here. Wherever here is."

He said those last words sullenly.

"You're in Roarr's bedroom inside my house," I told him. "But you can't stay here."

"He can't?" Roarr said.

I caught his eye over Fjolnir's shoulder and shook my head. I didn't want Fjolnir that close to Esja. But I wasn't going to say that out loud.

Then I turned to Skefill. "I want you and Raggi to stay with Fjolnir. All day and all night. I know this is a hardship. You're both tired, and you'll have to sleep in shifts to keep a watch over him. But you absolutely must."

"I've missed more sleep than this before," Skefill said.

"We'll see it done," Raggi said.

"You'll have to be off the patrols tomorrow night," I said with a glance to Thormund, who just gave me a nod. He'd pass the word along to his father. "I need you to keep Fjolnir somewhere safe, but outside of town."

Only, where? Anything I could think of was too far outside of town. And I really didn't want to offer up my cabin in the woods. That was my special place.

"My house," Raggi said. "My roommates can stay elsewhere for as long as we need."

"That will work," I said. "Keep him there until I say otherwise. I will be there at sunrise tomorrow, if not sooner."

"We can tie him to a chair if that helps," Skefill said. He smirked at his cousin's shocked expression, as if to say he was only joking.

But then he shot a look at me that said he absolutely was not.

"I'll leave that to your discretion," I said as mildly as I could.

Then I stepped back so Skefill could extend a hand and help his cousin off the bed.

"You really trust them?" Roarr asked me in a low hiss the minute the three of them were out of earshot.

"They'll do it," Thormund said before I could even answer.

"They will," I agreed. "You should get some rest now that your bed is free. I will doubtless need you to be more alert than I later, when I get back with Esja."

"Get back? From where?" he asked.

"From seeing my mormor," I said.

Because there was no way I was getting a wink of sleep before she had been brought up to date with everything that had happened on that ship.

I had no idea what to do next with Esja. But I really hoped my grandmother did.

CHAPTER NINETEEN

AFTER I FINISHED TELLING my grandmother everything that had been happening up in Villmark since I'd seen her last, she was quiet for a very long time. She just gazed at Esja, who tried hard not to fidget under the intensity of that gaze.

"And you remember nothing of any of this?" Mormor asked at length.

"I remember going out on the longship," Esja said. "And I remember coming back on the longship. It's just the bit where everyone else met a dragon that I don't really remember at all."

Right. The bit where she had rolled her eyes back into her head and spoke to us all in a language older than time. That bit.

Not that I said any of that out loud. I just waited for my grandmother to speak.

We were in my grandmother's newly built cabin, an almost exact replica of her previous cabin. Despite that newness, it felt exactly like the place I had spent all those childhood summers. The flagstone floors were as coolly soothing underfoot as ever. The fireplace with its Nordic carving in all the wood ornamentation was currently not hosting a fire, but the remains of one sat crumbling on the grate.

And, as always, the air smelled of waffles and coffee. The coffee we were all three sipping as we talked. But the waffles had not made an appearance. Perhaps the smell lingered from the day before, or even the day before that. But the vanilla and toasted batter smell was still strong in the air.

Or, you know, maybe I was just really hungry. I had gotten Esja out of bed and hustled her down the ridge into Runde without stopping to eat anything.

And whatever number of cups of coffee I was on, it was about six too many on an empty stomach. My hands were practically trembling from the combined power of exhaustion and strong caffeine.

"This light that came out of Fjolnir's mouth, you saw it go back to the lake?" my grandmother asked me at last.

"Not specifically," I admitted. "I just assumed. I mean, where else would it go?"

"Into another person in Villmark?" my grandmother said sharply.

"Oh," I said. Because, yeah. That was a real possibility. One I should have thought of on my own.

Mjolner and I should've kept chasing that light. I mean, we didn't know which way it had gone, but we could've at least split up and tried to find it.

"Too late now," my grandmother said, as if reading my mind. Then she sighed heavily. "There's nothing else to be done, I'm afraid. I'll have to close the mead hall."

"Close the mead hall?" I all but shrieked. That sounded so extreme. And so not related to the actual problem plaguing Villmark.

"Just for one night, dear," she said with a soft smile. "You'll need me up in Villmark, I think. And I need to see for myself just what is going on up there."

"So you truly have never felt the presence of anything in the lake?" I asked.

"I have," Esja said. "Before I went out of my head, I felt like something was watching us. Something under the water."

My grandmother looked at her steadily but said nothing.

"It isn't new, that thing we saw," I said. "It's been there for at least a year."

"Oh, I'm sure it's been there longer than that," my grandmother said, looking at the bottom of her empty coffee cup with a sigh. "To answer your question, no. I've never seen the thing you've described. Although I agree with you, it can't possibly be literally Nidhogg. That isn't conceivable. That would mean the beginnings of Ragnarok. And that I *would* sense."

"Still, it looked like a dragon," I said. "But a dragon the size of a spinosaurus."

"Hmm," was all my grandmother said. I got the feeling that all she knew about spinosauruses was that they were dinosaurs.

"Lake Superior is so deep," I said. "Do you think there's more than one down there?"

"What a horrific idea," Esja said with a shiver. And she didn't even remember the thing. She'd only heard me and the others describe it.

But my grandmother was already waving her hand dismissively. "No, not at all. I'm quite sure there's only one. And I believe it's been here for centuries. I think it was pursuing Torfa. I suppose it took time for it to find her again after she moved our ancestors across the planet by magic, bringing them from Norway to here."

"The way wasn't even open from the ocean to here until the canals were built," I said.

"Falls and rapids wouldn't really hold back a creature like what you saw," Mormor said. "It would find a way. And it had her magical scent. But there is no record of it ever being seen in or near Villmark. No fishing expeditions report anything like it. Nothing."

"So you think it's been here for centuries, but just lurking at the bottom of the lake?" I asked.

"Biding its time, yes," my grandmother said.

"Until now?" Esja asked. "What's changed now?"

My grandmother fell into silent thought again.

"Fjolnir was out with the other fishermen, and he sensed it," I said quietly. "Maybe he lured it somehow?"

"No, they went out after the attacks started happening," Esja reminded me.

"Yes, but he said he's felt something down there for quite some time," I said. "I mean, he's seventeen, so his idea of a long time is probably a little… off. But still. It's more than a few days ago."

"So maybe he did summon it?" Esja said. "But he doesn't remember doing it now?"

"It's a theory," I said.

"How terrible," Esja said. "To do things and not remember doing them is bad enough when you didn't even do anything horrific."

"We can't put this all on Fjolnir," my grandmother said as she got up to refill her cup from the pot still on her stove.

"I'm not saying he's to blame," I said. "I just think maybe he is the way into the town, somehow. Maybe not willingly, but that dragon thing is using him to get inside."

Esja looked like she was about to nod her agreement, but then tipped her head to one side and looked at my grandmother instead.

"No, it doesn't quite fit," my grandmother said as she poured a measure of cream into her coffee. "Fjolnir wasn't in Villmark when Brana was taken. And there are seven witnesses to attest to that fact."

"Oh," I said, suddenly deflated. "Right."

"Something complicated is going on," my grandmother said. "But then, that's why I'll be in the village commons tonight. I need to see this thing for myself. It's good that you have Fjolnir under guard, but I don't think that's going to stop that thing out in the lake from striking again. It will find a way."

"And then we'll chase the next floating ball of light back to the source," I said.

"One of us will," my grandmother said with a gleam to her eye. Like she was challenging me to a contest.

But just as soon as it was there, that gleam was gone again. She slid back into her chair at the table and looked at first me and then Esja before taking a sip from her cup.

"I'll be in the village commons, and the mead hall will be closed. But I have a different assignment for the two of you," she said.

"Anything," Esja said, more eagerly than I would've managed it if I had spoken first.

"The two of you are going to miss patrolling for a night," my grandmother said. "I need you both to stay by the ancestral fire."

"Valki will appreciate the opportunity to direct things from the commons and not from afar," I said.

"Yes, but the important thing is the two of you by that fire," she said.

And I had a sinking feeling I knew where she was going with this. And it was already making me so nervous.

But Esja just looked at my grandmother with her wide blue eyes and said, "I'm to be tasked with guarding the ancestral fire?"

"Yes," my grandmother said.

"I've only done, like, three patrols," Esja said.

"I know," my grandmother said.

"You want to see if she starts talking again," I said, and Esja's eyes went even wider as she finally understood. "But, Mormor, what good will that do? I still won't be able to understand her."

"Nobody understood me that first time either," Esja said. "When I set my clothes on fire. The last time I was just standing near the ancestral fire."

"Ingrid will be watching you this time," my grandmother said. "You won't set yourself on fire a second time."

"Yeah, but I don't see how I'm going to understand her either," I said. "Even if I knew what language she was speaking last time, there isn't any way I could learn it before tonight."

"No, obviously not," my grandmother said. "But I think, being near the ancestral fire, you'll be able to help Esja coax a more willing spirit to speak through her."

"You think there's been more than one?" Esja asked, horrified.

"I know there's been at least two," I told her. "The voice that spoke through you when we were coming home in the wagon from that well west and north of Villmark was very different from the one that was speaking on the longship."

"So you think you can get her back again? Or another one?" Esja asked. She sounded exhausted just saying the words.

"I don't know what I can do," I said, looking to my grandmother helplessly.

But she just shrugged and took another sip of her coffee before saying, "I don't know either. But the two of you need to figure this out together."

I looked down at my half-full cup of coffee, but opted not to sample any more of its bitter, now cold contents. I pushed it away and sat back in my chair with a sigh.

Esja was just staring down into her cup as if trying to divine from tea leaves. Which, given it was both coffee and still nearly full, would've been a bit of a trick.

But then she said, in the tiniest of voices, "Can Roarr be there too?"

My grandmother gave this a moment's consideration before saying, "No."

"Remember, he can see things when I can't sometimes," I put in.

"No," my grandmother said, more firmly this time. "What value Roarr has, it won't come into play by the fire. You won't miss seeing Esja change any more than he would. And I need him elsewhere tonight."

"Okay," I gave in, then glanced over at Esja. Who, despite her early morning hour nap, was fighting a massive yawn. "I think the two of us should get some sleep before nightfall. If that's all right?"

"Yes, do that," my grandmother said. But she let out a sigh that told me without asking that she didn't see any sleep in her own future.

"Can we help you with anything first?" I offered.

"No, no," she said with a dismissive wave. "Run along. Get your sleep. Pay attention to your dreams. But be at the fire by sunset. Don't make me tell you to go there twice."

"We'll be there," Esja swore, her fist over her heart in a gesture as solemn as any of the Thors had ever done.

The corner of my grandmother's mouth twitched ever so slightly, but she held the smile back and just gave Esja a very grave nod.

Then the two of us were back out in the bright golden morning, bustling through a slowly waking Runde.

At least whatever was going on inside the lake, it wasn't threatening these people. Villmarkers were prepared for anything, even something very like a dragon that had been hunting their clan for centuries. But the people of Runde would be such easy pickings. And what could I or even my grandmother do to keep them safe?

Although I was starting to fear that the same was becoming true of Villmark too. As skilled as they all were with swords, axes and bows, those weren't the weapons to use in the fight that faced us now.

I only hoped my magic and my grandmother's would be enough.

It had to be.

CHAPTER TWENTY

THAT NIGHT, Esja and I sat alone in the cavern by the ancestral fire.

I had brought my art bag. Not just because I generally brought that with me everywhere I went. It was also because... well, it's not like I didn't understand why Valki spent so much time sharpening his weapons.

Just watching a fire got boring fast. Especially with the mead hall closed and no one passing by on their way down to Runde. Every Villmarker was either on patrol, or securely indoors with at least a group of others if not gathered inside the council hall with most of the town.

Because that night, there were more than just young families inside the council hall. After Fjolnir had nearly succeeded in pulling a grown woman out of her own kitchen, word had gotten around.

Everyone was armed with something, even if it was just a kitchen knife or a child's slingshot. And everyone was keeping an eye on everyone else.

If I was geared up for yet another night without sleep, at least I had lots of equally tired company.

But there wasn't really any comfort in that.

I idly sketched in a fresh sketchbook that I had brought with me.

Nothing even trying to be magical, just a little drawing of Thorbjorn as best as I could remember him.

It had been months since I'd seen him. But all the details that made him *him* were there at the forefront of my mind as I drew.

Esja, on the other hand, was taking our assignment very seriously. She sat on her three-legged stool, still wearing her weapons, although there wasn't likely to be anything here we'd have to fight with steel. She had her hands resting lightly on her knees.

And she was staring into those flames with an intensity that had me a little worried about the effects on her eyes. It couldn't be good, staring into a light source like that. And the heat was pretty intense. I imagined her eyeballs were drying out already.

But eventually she blinked hard, as if feeling what I was thinking, and sat back a little further on her stool.

Then she looked over at my sketchbook. I had an urge to cover up what I was doing, but fought it back down. She watched me draw for several long minutes without saying a word.

But then, out of nowhere, she asked, "What's it like? When you're drawing and you go into that fugue state? What does that feel like?"

I paused in my shading, smudging the graphite a little with one fingertip, before answering. "Why do you ask? I'm not in a fugue state now."

"I know," she said with a little laugh. "Your whole… everything is different when you're drawing with magical sight. It's pretty hard to miss. I know you're just drawing now for fun. Or, you know, because you miss him."

She trailed off for a moment, and I knew without asking that she was thinking of her brother, somewhere far off to the north. Maybe with Thorbjorn still, or maybe on his own. They had told me they'd part ways at some point, but neither had any idea of when that would be.

Or when they'd be back.

"Anyway, I was just wondering if it was like what happened to me on the ship," she said in a small voice.

"Oh," I said, still smudging the shadows I had roughed in with my pencil. "No, I don't think it's remotely like that."

"Okay, so what *is* it like?" she pressed.

"It's like I go to a place in the back of my own mind, I guess," I said musingly. I had never thought about how I would describe it before. "Or, sometimes, it's like I'm floating up above. In either case, I'm watching. I can see what I'm doing, and I can feel that I'm doing it. But mostly I'm watching to see what comes out on the page." I switched back to my pencil, adding details to the waves of Thorbjorn's hair. It would be longer now. It always was, when he was in the north.

"So you're always aware, then," she said almost glumly.

"No, actually," I admitted. "Sometimes I just wink out entirely, and when I come to, I look at pages and pages of things I don't even remember drawing."

"So that's a bit like what happened to me, then," she said. Heartened a little, I thought.

"Maybe," I said. "But maybe not. I mean, it still always feels like what happened, it was *me* doing it. I gather that's not how you felt after you came to on the ship."

"No," Esja said.

"I mean, I don't remember doing it. But it's art. And when I look at it, even if it's super rough or super refined, I can still tell it's my work. It has my style. Like even in an automatic state, it's still my skills crafting it all," I said.

"And I spoke a language I don't even know," Esja said. She had her chin on her hand now, still watching me draw, but with a much glummer attitude.

"Just because none of us recognized it doesn't mean you won't know it someday," I said. "And just because the whole process is out of control for you now doesn't mean you won't ever master it."

"Because you think it's Skuld I'm channeling," Esja guessed. "And Skuld is the future."

I paused in my drawing. I actually hadn't been thinking that at all. I was just talking.

And yet, it made a kind of sense. Time in the lore of our Norse ancestors was a little strange, at least to my modern thinking. The past was vast, and the future grew from that past. But the present was always almost just an illusion. Like it was never really there. It was just a frame in a long film reel. Like a still photograph, it wasn't real life.

That was another lesson of naudhr, I realized. The past laid a groundwork that didn't determine the future, but it certainly set the parameters within which the future had to exist.

And the present? It didn't really enter into it at all.

There were all our ancestors back to the dawn of time. Back to Ginnungagap, when there was just fire and ice.

And there were our descendants, who would carry on the hamingja of our families. Until Ragnarok, when everything would end before beginning again in some new form.

But the present? Still not really a major thing.

And yet, perhaps it was just my modern mind, but it still felt to me like the only thing I could really know *was* the present. Everything else was memory or guesswork.

"I don't know," I said to Esja at last. "I think some of those deeper mysteries will always be beyond my ability to grasp."

"I doubt that very much," Esja said.

"Well, thanks," I said.

But I still had doubts. So, so many doubts.

We sat in silence for quite some time, me adding more and more details to my portrait, Esja just watching me draw.

Then she said, tentatively, "So, this fugue state. It's different than when you were controlled by Halldis. Right?"

"Yes," I said without a moment's thought. "That was very different. I was, if anything, more aware than I am in the fugue state. I was trapped inside my own body. And it wasn't like I was in the back of my mind or anything. No, I was totally and completely there. I just couldn't stop what I was doing. No matter how badly I wanted to."

"So that's different too," she said.

"I think so."

She sighed, as if she had been hoping I'd say something else. But before I could ask what she was thinking, she said, "Was it the same for Roarr as it was for you? That feeling of being trapped helpless inside your own body?"

"I don't know," I admitted. "My grandmother says she's never been able to figure out just how much Roarr was aware of what was happening. Or how much he was doing without coercion. Because he was already in too deep to back out or something."

"I don't think he did anything bad without being controlled," Esja said.

"I wish I could be so sure," I said. "I've come to trust him in the year that I've known him. But I'll never be sure of what he did back then."

Esja looked at the fire for a moment, her chin still propped on her hand. "I don't think he could help it. That's not who he is."

"It might not be who he is now," I said. "But it might be who he was, then."

Esja just gave me a soft, "Hmm."

And I went back to my drawing.

But then she said, "It's going to be Skefill's sister this time."

"What's that?" I asked her conversationally.

But then I realized the voice I had heard coming out of her for just that last sentence wasn't her usual speaking voice. It was deeper, more sonorous. And it was speaking in a very formal version of Villmarker Norse. Not accented exactly, just very, very posh.

"Esja?" I said softly.

"Don't say her name now," she told me. "Not now."

"Skuld?" I said, even more softly.

But she just waved that name away as if the mere sound of it were a great annoyance to her.

"Listen to me, because there isn't much time," she said.

I just stared into her eyes, transfixed. They were Esja's eyes, perfectly normal, if a little too intensely beautiful a shade of cornflower blue.

"Skefill's sister is the next target, but you will get there in time to save her," she said.

"She's in the council hall with the other families," I said, knowing that for a certainty. I shoved my book back inside my art bag.

But Esja, still seated on her three-legged stool, caught my arm in a grip of iron and held me there.

"No, don't go to her. She's fine. You need to get to Raggi."

"Raggi?" I repeated.

"Raggi is who you need to save first. Go!"

She released me with a little push, not enough to move my grounded feet but enough for me to be turned away for half a second.

And when I turned back, it was definitely Esja again, blinking up at me with a thousand new questions in her blue eyes.

"Ingrid?" she said. "Did something just happen again? I feel so funny. Like I lost time again. How much time did I lose?"

"Just a moment, really," I assured her.

"What did I say?" she asked. "Tell me, please."

"No time," I told her. "We need to get to Raggi's cabin west of town. We're going to have to run."

"But, the fire?" she said.

"We have to leave it," I said. "It'll be fine."

I had nothing to back up that statement. Nothing but a feeling deep in my bones that it was true.

But Esja looked from me to the flames, and as if the flames themselves had somehow given her the nod, she just grabbed her cloak to go with me.

I slung my bag across my body, then we jogged out of the cavern, up the natural stone steps to the meadow above.

The moon was still a sliver. Although it was high in the sky, it illuminated nothing.

But it didn't matter. I knew the way well. I ran for all I was worth, ran through the stand of birch trees and on through Villmark proper. And Esja stayed close beside me, although I could tell this was mere politeness on her part. If she wanted to, she could've run far ahead of me. She could've left me in her dust.

We passed four different patrols, who all let us by with only a few shouted greetings that I was too out of breath to return.

Esja, following my lead, said nothing.

And we passed through the village commons. There was no sign of my grandmother anywhere in that open, cobblestoned square. But I didn't slow down to look more closely, let alone really investigate.

I just ran. We ran. We ran past Aldis's mead hall and through the first of the hills to the west of the village until we reached Raggi's little cabin.

To find it glowing with light.

CHAPTER TWENTY-ONE

MY INITIAL TERROR response soon calmed when I realized it wasn't magical light I was looking at. It was mere firelight, if an excessive amount of it. Like whoever was inside had stoked up the fireplace to the max, and then lit a bunch of lamps and maybe a couple of braziers besides.

Seriously, while it was constructed mostly of stone and sod, there was still enough wood at the door and doorframe—not to mention the furniture inside—that I marveled that the entire thing hadn't caught on fire already.

"Ingrid?" Esja said, confused at the slowing of my steps. "This is it, right? Where we were going?"

"This is it," I said.

"Who's inside?" she asked.

"Raggi," I said.

"Wait, I thought we were rescuing someone?" she said.

"We are," I said, but before I could explain further, something blocked out the light. A large figure was standing in the doorway, filling that space so tightly very little of the light beyond could reach us anymore.

"Raggi?" I called nervously.

But he didn't react to my voice. Not that I was even sure it was him. It was hard to tell from the silhouette of a large man in a cloak with the hood up. It could be nearly half of Villmark, potentially.

But then his head snapped to one side, as if he had just heard someone call out his name from somewhere off to the east.

Then he was running, but not towards us. It was at about a forty-five degree angle away from us. I pivoted and tried to chase after him, but I was really too winded from my run across town to work up to much of a sprint so quickly.

Esja, on the other hand, was still perfectly fresh. She launched from where we were standing on the edge of the road, flying through the air to land between Raggi and whatever his goal was.

He snarled at her, the sound like nothing human. But Esja was undeterred. She just drew both of her swords and shouted a mighty war cry at him.

He threw off his cloak, and I was finally certain it was Raggi, even by the dim light from the stars and the sliver of moon.

But he hadn't thrown off his cloak so that I could identify him. He had done it to free his own sword from the folds of the cloth. He swung that massive blade up and over his head with a bellow, then brought it crashing down on Esja's head.

I was already shrieking, but she was perfectly calm. She just brought those two swords up, catching the descending blade between them as if she were holding a huge pair of scissors.

Then she took a step back, letting his blade continue its arc down to the ground. But before he could pull it back up for a second attempt, she lunged in at him, cutting two long gashes through the leather of his jerkin.

Judging from the sudden hiss of his breath, they had cut a little of his flesh as well.

But Esja just stood with her swords at the ready, waiting to see what he would do next.

He took half a step back with a cry, pulling that monstrously huge sword back to lift it over his head again. And Esja was shifting her weight forward on the balls of her feet.

She was going to charge him. I could tell. She was just timing it for his most vulnerable moment, when that sword was at its highest point.

But I didn't think Raggi—even an apparently possessed Raggi, which I really hoped he was in that moment—could possibly miss twice.

I tried to cry out a warning, but before I could utter a syllable, Skefill was there. He had an axe in his hands, but he didn't wield it. He just drove a shoulder into Raggi's chest, so hard it knocked the breath from him.

Raggi staggered back, sword hanging limply from one hand.

"Yield!" Skefill commanded him. Although there was a touch of desperation in his voice. He really didn't want to hurt his friend.

But he would, if he had to.

And he didn't even know who Raggi had been going after, I would bet.

But Raggi ignored his command and his tone both, raising that sword once more before lowering his head to charge forward again.

But now there were three Esjas flowing around the hesitating Skefill to close in on Raggi. They danced around him, their swords catching more silvery moonlight than the moon was even putting out. It was like little jags of sideways lightning, shooting all around Raggi's form.

Some of those bolts were sword slashes striking home, to judge from the bellows of annoyance and pain that Raggi was emitting.

But then Skefill lunged in again. He made a move too quick for my eyes to see clearly, and then Raggi's long sword was sailing up into the air. It seemed to hang there for a moment before turning groundward, striking in the middle of the road hard enough to plunge deep into even that rock-hard earth.

And Raggi fell to his knees, smothered by the combined efforts of Skefill and three valkyries.

I admit it, it took way too long for me to figure out that it wasn't just Esja. Nilda and Kara were there, too. They had entered the fray while I was watching Skefill plead with his friend.

The three of them made short work of binding Raggi up tightly, but Skefill just stepped back, then turned to me.

"Something happened," he said.

"I gathered that," I said drily. "Did he take a boat out on his own?"

"No, nothing like that," Skefill said.

"Why don't we go inside and you can explain," I said, and turned towards the brightly lit, still open doorway.

"No!" Skefill said, catching my arm with both of his hands to keep me from heading towards the sod house.

"What's in there, Skefill?" I asked. I had the sudden horrid feeling that we had been too late. That somehow his sister was here and not at the council hall. Here, and dead, inside that tiny house.

But Skefill, still clutching my arm, took a deep breath and forced himself into a state of calm.

Or, relatively calm, anyway.

"It's probably safe for you," he said.

"Because I'm a volva?" I said.

"I think maybe just this thing only targets men," he said. "I mean, it's abducting women, but it's using men to do it. It isn't safe in there, with Fjolnir."

"Thormund and Roarr?" I asked.

"They aren't inside," he said. "They're with your grandmother. Nora Torfudottir."

"They're patrolling," Nilda said as she and Kara approached with Raggi bound between them. He was hanging limply from their grasp, and I could tell it was work for the two of them to keep him moving.

"The light left him," Esja told me. "I saw it go, but I couldn't chase it. It just disappeared too fast."

"Believe me, I know," I said to her. Then, "Where is my grandmother patrolling?" I asked Nilda.

"She wanted to see the places where we knew people went missing," Kara said. "I think they started on the north end and were going to end up outside the council hall."

"Good," I said. Then I glanced at Esja and then at Skefill. "Esja had a vision at the ancestral fire. She saw that Raggi was going to try to take your sister. We ran here first to stop him. But if that ball of light gets inside someone else, it's good that she's already there."

"But she might not be," Skefill said, suddenly pale.

"Go," I told him. "Go be with your sister and her family. We can take care of Raggi and Fjolnir from here."

He looked dubious, but only for a second. Then he was off running, sword still in his hand.

Which didn't seem wise, but he was gone too fast for me to call after him to put it away first.

"Inside?" Kara asked, bringing my attention back to her and her sister. They were starting to flag under Raggi's almost dead weight.

"Yes, get him in a chair and bind him to it," I said, letting them go through the doorway first.

Then Esja and I followed.

Fjolnir was there, apparently wide awake. He was tied to a chair but not gagged. He was also shivering, as if he had been caught outside in a snowstorm and had just reached the warmth of a fire.

A fire he was sitting awfully close to. But the warmth didn't seem to touch him.

"Fjolnir?" I said softly as I came closer.

"I didn't mean to," he said, mostly talking to his own feet.

"I know you didn't," I said. "Something is working through you, but not with your consent, I'm sure. Do you remember anything?"

"Skefill and Raggi were sitting with me," he said, his hair still blocking his eyes and face from my view. "They were telling me tales of their adventures on patrol. All made up, I'm sure. Just idle boasting. But I get it. They were just trying to cheer me up. To distract me."

"Then what happened?" I asked.

"I started to recite a poem," he said. "I don't know why. Something Raggi said just made me think of it. It's about a hunter who crosses a frozen lake. That's all. It's something one of our ancestors wrote, one of the original settlers who came over from Old Norway with Torfa. I learned it for school years ago. I just like it."

"You started reciting a poem about the lake?" Esja asked, her brow furrowed.

"Not *the* lake," Fjolnir said, finally tossing his hair back to glare at her, then shoot a pleading look my way. "It's just about *a* lake. It's a metaphor, right? About the still, calm mind of a hunter. I just liked it because it had really cool repeating sounds in it. And it was in Old Norse, so it sounded… well, old."

"Sure," I said. "But then what happened?"

"I don't know," he said, and returned his gaze to his own feet. "I don't remember the next bit."

"Do you remember seeing a light?" Esja asked, touching her lips as if wordlessly prompting him to think of his own mouth. But he wasn't looking at her, so the clue was lost on him.

"I don't know. I just kind of blinked, and Raggi was throwing my cousin around," Fjolnir said softly. "Then he ran out the door. I guess that's when you showed up. It all happened so fast."

"Did you picture *the* lake in your mind at all?" I asked. "When you were saying the poem, or after, during the bit that you don't remember?"

"Close your eyes and let your mind go quiet," Esja said, squatting in front of his chair to put her hands on his knees. "See what rises to the surface when your mind is still."

Fjolnir sat quietly for a dozen long, slow breaths.

Then he said, "Yeah. When I wasn't here, I was falling in the lake again. Falling, falling, falling."

Behind us, Nilda grabbed Raggi by the chin and rolled his head back so she could look into his face. But his eyes were glazed and unseeing.

"It might take him a minute to come back to us," I said.

"Not that he'll remember much when he *is* back," Nilda grumbled, and let his head roll forward onto his chest once more.

"Can you two guard these two?" I asked Nilda and Kara.

"Sure," Nilda said, and Kara nodded as well. "Are you going to catch up with your grandmother?"

I looked over at Esja, who gave me a curt nod.

"We are," I said. "And then, I think, we're going out onto the longship again. With a full crew, this time, though."

"Best of luck, Torfudottir," Kara said, with a quick tap of her fist against her chest in salute.

"I can find the spot again," Esja said as we headed back into town, traveling down the road in a quick walk, since I was definitely not up for more running yet.

"Are you sure?" I asked. But only because I didn't think I could find it again at all. Some random bit of water far, far from shore? No way I was finding that again. I had kind of hoped that Thormund, with his knowledge of the stars, would tell me that he could.

But Esja's nod in answer was one of total confidence. "Yes. I can feel it. What's out there. I don't think I'll lose myself again this time, but in case I do, I know you'll be prepared. And before that happens, I'll have gotten us close enough for it to matter."

"If you're sure you're ready to do this again?" I said.

But Esja just gave me another confident nod. "Yes," she said. "Yes, I think right now, I'm ready for anything."

I really wished that feeling was contagious. But at least this time, my grandmother would be with us.

I hoped that would make all the difference.

CHAPTER TWENTY-TWO

THIS TIME, when the longship left the harbor, it was my grandmother who worked the spells to part the waters and keep us hidden as we passed by the farms and houses of Runde.

And we had a full crew at the oars, so there was no need to raise the sail and summon magical winds. Given the energy every single one of us needed to burn off, and were vigorously doing so with every stroke of our oars, even the stiffest breeze would've been slower than the speed we were making over the gently chopping waters.

I was sharing an oar with Skefill, by my express choice. Esja and Roarr were working the oar just ahead of us, and Thormund was at the rudder. And my grandmother was behind us, sitting on the three-legged stool where she worked her magic.

The minute the shore had slipped far enough away behind us to the west, she let go with every bit of her power. We were encased in a sphere of bright golden light, brighter even than the spells that protected her mead hall.

But unlike her mead hall, every one of us could see these lights. They could feel her protection around all of us.

I think it made all of us row all the faster as Thormund guided the rudder. He only occasionally needed to shout out a question to Esja and adjust our course to the pointing of her arm.

Like I had suspected, he pretty well remembered where we had been.

I was a little worried about the amount of power my grandmother was throwing off. But I had never seen her so fiercely riled up in my life. I hadn't had time to get more than a few words out of her between the council hall and the boat harbor, but it had been enough to get the clear impression that whatever she had sensed while touring the crime scenes had left her absolutely enraged.

Which brought my thoughts back to my seatmate, Skefill. I had told him he'd be sitting with me when we'd boarded the ship, and he hadn't questioned it. Perhaps he already knew what I was going to ask him.

But he still waited for me to ask it. When we were past the mouth of the river, far enough out for the strokes of our oars to fall into an even rhythm, I finally spoke.

"Tell me what you saw," I said to him. "Raggi was too out of it to tell me anything, and Fjolnir's story is garbled and incomplete. But you were there the whole time. You saw everything. Tell me."

"We were telling tales, to keep the boy's mind off his worries," Skefill said. "He was taking it hard, the thought that he had done something that he couldn't remember. Possibly something truly terrible. It was eating at him. So we were boasting and laughing, and he seemed to be in brighter spirits for it."

"But he was tied up the entire time," I said.

"Yes, we never wavered in our watch over him," he said. "But then something Raggi said shifted the mood. Or Fjolnir's mood, anyway. He started reciting an old poem, one we all know from our childhood days. The driving rhythm of the words just gets inside your mind and won't stop running around and around."

"I'm familiar with that phenomenon," I said, deciding now wasn't the time to explain the concept of an "ear worm" to a Villmarker isolationist.

"It's a melancholy poem," Skefill went on. "And for a moment after he was done, we were all just quiet together. Then Raggi moved. I thought he was just going to put another log on the fire—"

"Yes, let's stop there. What was with all the fire?" I interrupted to ask.

"My idea," he said. "Fjolnir kept complaining that he felt cold, so cold. But even after the fire was blazing hot, he kept complaining. And I got the sense it wasn't so much warmth he was craving, but actual light. Like the shadows were bothering him when he'd catch them out of the corners of his eyes. So I lit everything Raggi had in his cabin that made any kind of light at all, and that seemed to help. That was before we started telling the stories."

"Okay," I said. That explained the borderline conflagration in the house, anyway. "Go on."

Skefill mulled for a moment, as if searching his memory for where he had left off. Then he said, "Raggi moved, I thought to put a log on the fire. But then he just sort of froze, bent over with an arm out towards the woodpile, but his eyes on Fjolnir's. Fjolnir was sitting kind of slumped over. You know the way he does? With his hair in his face?"

"I do," I said.

"Yeah, he was like that. So I couldn't see anything but his hair. But Raggi was looking into his face, and then it was like something moved out of Fjolnir and into Raggi. I didn't *see* anything. Not anything physical. But Fjolnir suddenly went from slouched like a teenager to fully collapsed, just kind of dangling from the ropes that we had tied him to the chair with. And Raggi jerked fully upright, like every muscle in his body had tensed all at once."

"Was there anything different about his eyes?" I asked. "Or did he say anything to you?"

"No, not a thing," Skefill said. "He just pushed me aside and charged over to the doorway. He stood there for what felt like forever, but then he went running outside. And you were there for the rest of it."

"You're sure you didn't see anything?" I pressed. "Not even something like a little ball of light moving from Fjolnir to Raggi?"

"No," he said, but slowly. "From where I was standing, the fire was behind them. And it was burning very brightly. I can't say for sure nothing was there. But I didn't see anything."

"Still, something that had been animating Fjolnir as he recited the poem moved over into Raggi and tried to run out the door and into the village," I said.

"I don't know what he was planning," Skefill said. "Not that I doubt you when you say he was heading to my sister. It's just, he didn't say anything to me at all. He didn't even respond when I called his name."

"This is it," Esja said suddenly.

Thormund gave the command for us all to stop rowing, and the ship slowed. Not quite to a halt, the motion of the waves was still moving us about. But without the sail up and snapping in the breeze, the lapping of the water against the hull of our longship was the only sound we could hear.

Everything else was completely silent.

My grandmother got to her feet, although she maintained the sphere of her power around us all. But I could see it was wearing on her. She wasn't going to be able to keep this up for long.

But she gave no sign of any intention to drop it. She just walked fore until she reached Esja's side, then took Esja by the arm and led her to the prow.

After a moment's hesitation, I followed them. The three of us leaned over the side as far as we dared and stared down into the water.

Even if the bottom of the lake hadn't been so very far below us, I doubted we'd have been able to see a thing. The surface of the water reflected the glow from my grandmother's magic far too strongly.

I gave up first, standing straight to scan the horizon in what I already knew would be a futile gesture.

Then my grandmother, still leaning over the side, glanced over at Esja.

"It's gone, isn't it?" she asked.

"I don't sense it here," Esja said, and straightened up.

"If it were here, I suppose you'd be in that altered state again," I said. Esja just shrugged. We had no way of knowing that for sure.

My grandmother was still peering down into the water, her eyes narrowed down into slits and focused on a point far beyond the glimmering surface.

Then finally she too straightened up with a sigh.

"It's moved on," she said.

"You're sure?" I asked.

"I can see its lair from here, and it's definitely abandoned now," she said.

"You can see—" I started to say, incredulously.

But Esja talked over me. "Abandoned for good? Or will it come back?"

"That I cannot say," my grandmother said. "Abandoned for a time, anyway, I should think. We are safe, for now."

"Safe?" I repeated. I wasn't even sure what that word meant anymore.

But my grandmother just made a quick gesture with her hand, and her sphere of power winked out in an instant.

And we were all plunged into darkness.

The sliver of the moon was making its way towards the western horizon now, and the stars were as dim as ever.

But then I saw something else. A different light reflecting on the water. I squinted at it, trying to figure out what its source was. Was that wave of water reflecting a full moon that wasn't even in our sky?

I mean, I had seen stranger things. Once, I had even traveled through time.

And yet, I didn't think that's what this was. Not a reflection. Something luminescent, maybe?

"What *is* that?" Esja said, having noticed me staring at something and followed my gaze to see it for herself.

"Let's row out that way," my grandmother said, pointing so that Thormund knew which way she meant.

"I don't think the others see it," Esja said.

"I see… something," Roarr said from where he was manning his oar alone. "It's like a reflection of a star that isn't in the sky?"

"Something like that," I said. But I thought he had the scale wrong. It looked bigger than a reflected star to me.

But my grandmother was already leaning out over the side, her hand extended as we slowly glided up to it.

My first thought was that she was doing this much too soon. We still had a long way to go to reach it, and any random wave could throw her overboard while she was perched so precariously.

But before I could say a thing, she was scooping it up into the palm of her hand.

And I realized that the thing I had seen wasn't very far away. It just wasn't all that big. *I* had gotten the scale all wrong.

But a light on water? It's hard to get a sense of the size of a thing that almost doesn't exist physically.

My grandmother turned to Esja and me with the flickering light cupped in both of her palms.

"It's losing power," she said with a smile. "Do you see?"

She gestured for us to lean in closer. Like she was showing us a baby bird she had rescued after it had fallen out of its nest.

It looked like a living thing. Like a living, transparent thing of light.

I knew there were jellies in Lake Superior, invasive species that were carried through the locks with the cargo ships.

But this didn't look like any jelly I'd ever seen in an aquarium, let alone in the lake itself.

"What is it?" I asked. But in a whisper, as if I were afraid speaking aloud might harm the thing.

"It's what was inside Fjolnir and Raggi and most probably others," she told us. "It's been moving from host to host. It's where our missing Villmarkers have gone."

"But it's so tiny," Esja said. She was whispering too.

"The dragon was filling this ball with its own draconian magic. But this time, when this ball flew out here to get another charge, the dragon was gone," my grandmother said. "That's why it looks so tapped out. Its power is truly fading."

"Is it a living thing, then?" I asked.

"Not at all," my grandmother said. Then she carried it back to the three-legged stool. Gently, again like it was an injured baby bird. She picked up her walking stick, then she went fore again. She set the ball of dying light down in the middle of the boat between the two rows of benches filled with rowers and just behind the mast.

Then she touched it, just the softest of nudges, with her walking stick.

Which, I was very slow to realize, was more than a mere walking stick. I mean, in the year since I'd known my grandmother was a volva, I had never once seen her use the thing for magic. Although she did carry it with her everywhere she went. I *had* noticed that.

But at the touch of the tip of her walking stick to that apparently squishy ball, it at first gave like it was a dumpling made of raw, soft dough.

Then it burst like a soap bubble.

A familiar rush of cold wind blew through me. A wind that wasn't a wind. The smell it carried with it was so much more intensely lake smell than the actual water all around us.

And four people were suddenly huddled together in the middle of the boat.

Three I knew only by description. A woman in her mid twenties. Another in her eighties. And a third in her late thirties.

But the fourth, I knew from personal acquaintance.

It was Brana.

CHAPTER TWENTY-THREE

WE WRAPPED the three women and young Brana in blankets, and the rest of the crew started rowing for shore with all possible speed.

But my grandmother, Esja and I stayed with the huddled women, waiting for them to recover enough from their shock to talk to us.

I wished we had thought to bring hot beverages with us, or even something to eat. But we hadn't expected to return with all of our missing Villmarkers on board.

Brana, the last taken, seemed to recover first. She was shivering in the woolen folds of her blanket when a moonbeam glinted off of one of the plastic butterflies still clipped to her braid. And she looked up at me and then Esja with wide eyes.

"Fulla?" she asked.

"Fulla is fine," I assured her. "Very worried about you, but fine. You'll see her in the council hall just as soon as we get to shore."

"My children," the middle-aged woman who had to be Geira Palnisdottir said.

"Both fine," I said. "And your husband. Honestly, now that we have the four of you back, everyone in Villmark is fine."

"Thank the gods," the older woman, Dalla Leifsdottir, said.

Then the younger woman, Vigdis Olafsdottir, shook herself as if sloughing off an irritating weight. "What exactly happened?" she asked me sharply.

"I was hoping you could tell me," I said. "The last we knew about you, you were leaving Ullr's hall. I gather you were alone?"

"Yeah, only someone who thought they were funny was following me in the shadows," Vigdis said with a fierce scowl.

"Did you see who?" I asked.

"Just a shadow moving through shadows," she said. "I called out to them, but they refused to come out."

"Was it a big shadow or a smaller shadow?" Esja asked. "I mean, do you think it was someone like Thormund here, or more like a kid? Or a teenager?"

"I couldn't tell," Vigdis said. But then she pondered a minute before saying, "It was someone… No, never mind."

"No, go on. What were you going to say?" I asked.

"I was going to say, it was someone dark and scary," she said. Then barked out a laugh as if at her own expense. "I guess I got a little jumpy. But it was like a nightmare, like from back when I was a kid. Some dark, scary stranger waiting to grab me. Silly."

"I had the same impression," Dalla said. "Only I didn't find it silly."

"I didn't see anything," Geira said. "It all happened so fast. One minute I was setting a ball down on the steps of my back porch, and the next it was like I was up in the sky, inside the Northern Lights."

"It was just like that," Brana said. She sounded both awestruck, but also relieved. Like it was good to know she hadn't been alone in her experience.

"Did you see more than a shadow?" I asked Dalla, who was looking pensive, as if pondering her last words still.

"No," she said slowly. "No, it was just that feeling like something was stalking me, something from a nightmare. I realize that's not literally what it was. But it was like there was something out there, and this dark scary stranger was what it was pretending to be."

"But definitely not a teenager," Esja said.

I flinched but didn't hush her. Although on my own, I wouldn't have done anything so much like what in the modern world they'd call "leading the witness."

"If it helps," Thormund said from where he was still steering our ship, "the person I attempted to tackle in the alley the other night definitely wasn't Fjolnir."

"Not the right size?" I asked.

"That, but also I asked him about it later," Thormund said. "It's certainly possible that he doesn't remember everything he's been up to. But I don't think he was lying about not being in that alley. And, no, the man I was grappling with was definitely much larger."

"So we still have a stalker loose in Villmark?" I said, sitting back on my heels with a frustrated sigh.

"I don't think so," my grandmother said. "That isn't the impression I got from visiting all the places where you women were taken."

"What did you see?" Dalla asked.

"What I saw lines up nicely with what you just told us," my grandmother said to her. "Something was pretending to be something else. Whatever that gelatinous ball of light was that I just burst to release you all, it was disguising itself as something predatory as it sneaked up on you all."

"Then it was coming back out to the lake to recover its magical energy before returning again to take another victim," Esja said. Then she looked at me. "That's why you kept seeing lake imagery. This thing is *of* the lake."

"Like the other artifacts that keep turning up in our town are of the north," my grandmother muttered, if mostly to herself.

"And it's been hiding in Villmark inside the body of Fjolnir," I said. "When it wasn't an invisible wind. I don't think Fjolnir attacked any of you, not physically. Not on his own. And I don't think he deliberately put anyone in danger. He just didn't know. But he, by his own admission, spends a lot of time out on his family's fishing boat staring down into the depths. Because he knew something was down there. And he couldn't look away from it, even if he never quite saw it."

"And as he looked down into the depths, something down there was looking up at him," Esja said. Then she shivered, as if a downpour of icy water was dancing down her spine.

"It can get out of the barrier on its own, but to get back inside, it needs a host to hide inside of," my grandmother said.

"Can we fix that?" I asked.

"No," she said darkly. "I will not make that barrier impassable to the people of Villmark. So long as I live, every Villmarker will always be free to come and go as they choose. Changing that... would be worse than the alternative."

"Even if the alternative is predators stalking us inside our own town?" Esja asked.

"Even if," my grandmother agreed.

"We have patrols," I said. "And we can maybe find a way to detect things like this without changing the barrier."

I looked at my grandmother, but she just shrugged.

"So we still need to hide indoors after dark?" Brana asked.

"No way I'm doing that," Vigdis said with a dismissive sniff.

"Well," I said. "The thing that got you all is the very definition of unique. And we burst it letting you all out. You're safe from that, I can say that for sure."

"Maybe stay armed," Esja recommended, touching the hilt of one of her swords.

"Groups are safer," I added.

They all nodded their agreement with those points. But there was a gleam in Vigdis' eye that told me everything we had said was very much going in one ear and out the other.

"Fjolnir didn't mean to do it, then?" Brana asked shyly.

"No, I don't think he did," I said. "But my grandmother and I will be watching him closely just to be sure nothing is wrong with him."

"And I," Roarr added, letting me know that everyone on the ship was apparently hanging off our every word.

"And I," Thormund said. Although I had already known he was listening in.

We rode on in silence through the night for the rest of the way home. But once we were close enough to the waterfall for the crash of falling water to mostly cover her words, Esja turned to speak close to my ear.

"The dragon is gone, and the jelly ball thing is no more," she said. "So we're safe now? It's all over?"

She pulled back to look at me, real concern in her eyes.

I nodded first, then leaned close to her own ear. "As safe as we can ever be."

That seemed to hearten her more than the same words would've heartened me. But if she was aspiring to honorary Mikkelsen valkyrie status, she would have to be, by definition, much braver than I was.

Still, I had questions.

Like, was that dragon the thing using the magic jelly ball? Or was it merely helping out some other, more fearsome being?

Because we had driven it off all too easily for my taste. And I didn't like the feeling it was biding its time to return when least expected.

But if it were reporting to some larger being, was it something deeper down in the lake?

Or was it in league with the strange women of the north?

Because I already hated the feeling I had from them, that they were biding their time to appear at the moment of their own choosing. A moment when they could wreak maximum havoc.

But perhaps the idea that chilled me most of all was that it was kind of both. Something lurked in the bottom of the lake, and in the north both. And it was closing in on us.

And whatever was its true form, I had yet to see it.

But Esja was watching my face too closely for me to let a single feeling I was having find its way into a micro-expression that might give my dark thoughts away. So I just gave her as reassuring of a smile as I could.

Then we both got up to help the four victims off the ship to rejoin their families and friends up at the council hall.

It was bound to be a heck of a party. But all I longed for was my own quiet house. My cat and my bed. And all the uninterrupted hours I needed to finally get some restful sleep.

CHAPTER TWENTY-FOUR

It took me a couple of days of sleeping at night and waking in the morning before I felt really human again.

It took a little longer for me to wrap my head around everything that had happened.

I mean, everything had ended about as well as could be hoped.

Esja didn't have another speaking in dead languages episode, and none of the ones she had had this time had led her to do any harm. So that was good, even I had to admit that.

Esja, on the other hand, thought it was all marvelous. She had been feeling stronger since leaving her family home to the south of Vill-mark, I knew that. And she had certainly looked healthier.

But on the fourth or fifth day after we'd come back from the last trip on the longship, I found her in my garden practicing with her swords. The ones I had seen her fight Raggi with. And I finally noticed something that should've been clear to me much sooner if I'd been paying attention.

"When did you get so good with those?" I asked her. "I know you said the Mikkelsens have been teaching you, and Skefill and Roarr have been sparring with you. But it's more than that. Isn't it?"

She finished one last move with a touch of flourish, putting a foot on the stone bench at the back of my garden and using it to leap and twist through the air to land with both swords extended. A very unnecessarily parkour fighting move.

Then she sheathed both her swords and mopped at her brow before answering.

"Yeah, I think it was after I almost set myself on fire?" she said. "I still don't remember what I was saying or anything about what happened at all. But after that, I've just felt stronger. And it's like my muscles have memories of training I don't even remember doing."

"And it's still there? That muscle memory?" I asked.

"As strong as ever," she said, and drew one of her daggers to spin it around in her fingers. The movement was too quick even for my eyes to follow. She tossed it up into the air, caught it deftly by the hilt, then sheathed it again with a grin. "I can't explain it. But I *do* like it."

"I can see why," I said, returning her grin. But then I had to get serious again. "No more visions?"

"No," she said with a careless shrug. "I've even done extra shifts guarding the ancestral fire, either with Nilda or with Kara. But nothing." She bounced on her toes, as if eager to get back to her workout. "I'll tell you if that changes. You know that, right?"

"I know," I said.

I went back to my art station to look over the sketches I had been doing over the last few days. Some of them had been in a semi fugue state—I was still too tired to try for full magic—but none of them were giving me any sense of alarm.

Esja had survived her second burning, and her second channeling of a spirit of a Norn.

But she still had one left to go.

I hoped the last would be as painless as the second, but hoping was definitely Plan B.

Plan A was being prepared.

And for that, I was still relying on Roarr helping me keep an eye on Esja. Which he was eager to do.

But lately, he was equally eager to take off when I was going to be with Esja long enough for him to do his own thing. Although how that other thing was any kind of break for him, I didn't understand.

Because the other thing he was doing was spending time with young Fjolnir.

I knew Roarr could bond with him like none of the rest of us could. Fjolnir had been under the influence of that magic longer than anyone, and while in the end no one had been seriously hurt, he still had all the feelings about the ways he was used.

And no one knew more about what that was like than Roarr.

Still, knowing what Fjolnir got out of it didn't really explain how rewarding Roarr was finding the effort. Because Fjolnir, despite all of Roarr's attentions, remained as sullen as ever. Maybe even more so. And he spared no one his disdain, not even Roarr.

But Roarr just let it wash over and past him and kept focusing on the real Fjolnir behind it all.

Like, I suppose, he wished everyone else did with him.

It made me nervous, the two of them spending all the time together that Roarr could spare. It could be a good thing for both of them, sure.

But it could too easily slide into a relationship that brought out the worse in both of them. And I was afraid *that* would be something none of us recognized until it was far too late.

Surprisingly, it was Thormund who insisted I just let it be. No one else was disappearing from the streets of Villmark. The nights were safe, and the days were as pleasantly golden as ever. I didn't need to borrow trouble from a future that might not ever come to pass.

Perhaps he was right. But I only really relented when he promised me he would keep an eye on Roarr and Fjolnir both.

And so would Skefill. Who was actually stopping by my house every few days, and not just pretending to see me as a pretext for seeing Esja. No, he made a point of reporting in to me how his cousin Fjolnir was doing, and how the patrols were going.

Not that he had to. I wasn't part of the new rank structure that oversaw all the patrols now.

But the reason there even was a new rank structure to the patrols was because I wouldn't let Valki say no to me when I told him we needed one. And sure, each of his sons were given the rank just under his.

But so were Raggi and Skefill. And unlike the Thors, the two of them were always in town.

Neither of them officially thanked me, or acted like they had gotten a thing less than they had earned.

Still, I knew they were grateful. Skefill stopping by was one clue. Raggi not sneering the moment he saw me approaching was a strong second clue.

Being considered the equal to the Thors? That really was a big deal in Villmark. And while nothing about their lifestyles changed much—they still fished, patrolled, and hung out in Aldis' mead hall to the exclusion of pretty much any other activities—I knew they basked in their new status.

But it was like letting Roarr be Fjolnir's mentor of sorts. I just really hoped I wasn't going to come to regret it.

I was still stewing about all these things seven days after we'd returned from the lake when there was another late morning knock on my door.

As I walked down my long hallway to answer it, I was equal parts apprehensive that we had been wrong about everything and someone else had disappeared in the night, and wishful that maybe, just maybe, Thorbjorn was back.

When I opened the door and saw my grandmother standing there with her walking stick in one hand and a bag of fast food in the other, it was literally the last thing I ever expected to see.

"Are you going to invite me in?" she asked when the moment had dragged on far too long.

"Do I even have to?" I asked as I stepped back to let her into my mudroom. "I remind you, this is actually your house."

"Not anymore," she said, pronouncing each syllable distinctly.

But then she held up the bag of food. The smell of French fries was overwhelming, and my stomach growled loudly. "I thought after so long on this side of the barrier, you might be craving a little of the world you've left behind."

"Is that a cheeseburger in there?" I asked, even as my stomach growled more loudly than before.

"And a vanilla milkshake," she said. "I know it's been a few years since I took you to a drive-through, but I think I remember your favorite order."

I took the bag from her and all but ran into my kitchen to sit down with it at my table. She came through the doorway just as I was unwrapping the cheeseburger.

"It's still warm," I said.

"Must be magic," she said with a twinkle to her eye.

"And this is still cold," I said, pulling out the milkshake and stabbing the straw through the hole to take a long pull. It wasn't melted at all. I could barely get a bit of ice cream out of it through the straw.

It was perfection.

"Wait," I said even as I squeezed one of the ketchup packets out onto the corner of the burger's wrapper. "Is this some kind of bribe?"

"What would I need to bribe you to do?" she asked as she sat down across from me, putting her chin on her hands to watch me eat.

"This is out of nowhere," I said. "Why?"

She just shrugged, then gestured for me to try the fries. They were crisp and hot and salted exactly the right amount.

Yeah, it had to be magic. But it was the magic of the modern world.

"I guess I was feeling homesick," she said. "And I thought you might be feeling homesick, too."

"This is great," I said. "And you're right, I didn't even realize how much I was missing this. But what are *you* homesick for? You can walk up here anytime you like, you know."

"I guess it's more homesick for the past," she said. "Our little adventure out on the ship, I haven't done anything like that in years. And as exhausting as it was, I doubt I ever will again. But it was a nice little adventure all the same."

"It kind of fizzled out at the end," I said.

"You were hoping to fight a dragon?" She asked me with one arched brow.

I just shrugged, my mouth full of cheeseburger.

I mean, kind of?

But she understood my meaning without me having to explain it. She sighed pensively then said, "Well, either way. I promise it's for the best. Even you and I together are not ready to face that foe yet. Maybe not ever. Nobody wants to bring about the end of the world, do they?"

"You think if we fought it, we'd cause the end of the world?" I asked.

She chewed at her lip for a moment. "The two are linked. That's orlog, right?"

I fought the urge to groan. This was becoming a lot like a conversation with Haraldr, where I struggled to understand concepts that I almost, but didn't quite, grasp.

Like orlog. Which was like fate or karma. Except for all the ways where it wasn't like those things at all.

"That dragon isn't Nidhogg, though," I said.

"No, but dragons are dragons," my grandmother said. "You never face one when you can safely avoid it. Nothing is ever the same after facing a dragon as it was before you tried to face it, even if you can call the match a victory. No, the correct path is always to delay, delay as long as you can."

"But this dragon was taking our people," I said.

"Until it stopped," my grandmother said.

"But *why* did it stop? Because it knew we were on to it? Doesn't that sound like it was maybe a little afraid of us?"

"Of course it's a little afraid of us," my grandmother said. "I'm sure somewhere out there, when dragons meet, they council each other that you never face a volva when you can safely avoid it. Because nothing is ever the same after that confrontation as it was before. Nothing scores a victory against us without losing more than they bargained to in the process."

"So it backed off, but it isn't gone," I pointed out.

She said nothing, so I just turned my attention back to my cooling fries.

"I don't know exactly what kind of magic that dragon was using. It wasn't dragon magic as I know it. I've been studying and meditating and... doing my own things," she finished vaguely, with a little gesture that told me that questions about that would not be welcome.

But then she went on. "Something else gave that glowing thing to that dragon. It wasn't a spell, per se. It was another artifact. This time not metal jewelry or the like. It was some kind of goo, so I'm going with alchemy. Which I've never studied at all, so where does that leave us?"

I sighed as I poked my straw up and down in my milkshake, needlessly mixing it up as it hadn't had a chance to separate, before taking a sip. "The same place as ever," I said for her. "Something from the north is coming for us. It's trying to use whatever it can find lying around to get past our defenses. Only now there's also a dragon."

"There was always a dragon," my grandmother said. "The difference now is that we *know* there's a dragon."

"You make it sound like that's a good thing," I said.

"It's better than not knowing there's a dragon," she said.

Well, she had me there.

"Anyway, I just wanted to bring you a little treat," she said as she put both palms flat on my table to leverage herself back up to her feet. "It wasn't a *bribe*. I was just remembering a simpler time, when you were little and your mother let me have you for entire summers at a time. And we would drive up to Grand Marais just to get you this little... um. Taste of home."

I grinned at that. "You can't blame me for thinking this was special St. Paul food. I never left St. Paul except to come to Runde. And there's no fast food in Runde," I said.

"You had a television," she pointed out.

"I was..." I trailed off, uncertain.

"Six," she said. "Which was old enough."

"Do you know what I think?" I said as I got up to walk with her to the door.

"What do you think?" she asked, clearly humoring me.

"I think you loved fast food just as much as I did, and I was just your handy excuse to indulge," I said.

Then I handed her the remaining half of my milkshake.

She finished pulling on her second hiking boot, then took the waxed paper cup from me with a satisfied gleam to her eye.

I watched her go, walking and sipping, her stick thumping on the cobblestones beside her with each step.

The food had been decadently filling in that momentary way that fast food so often was.

But it didn't make me homesick. Not even a little.

As she turned right at the commons and disappeared from my field of view, I just remained standing in my front gate, watching the passing throngs of Villmarkers heading south to the market or north to the commons where some sort of craft fair had sprung up spontaneously because the weather was persisting in being so insanely gorgeous.

This was my home now. And I wouldn't trade it for anything.

Even if, as always, I missed Thorbjorn and Loke. That was an ache that never faded.

But someday, and hopefully someday soon, that would change.

Someday soon, they'd be there with me. And my home would be complete.

But in the meantime, I had art to do, and runes to study. And my easel was calling to me.

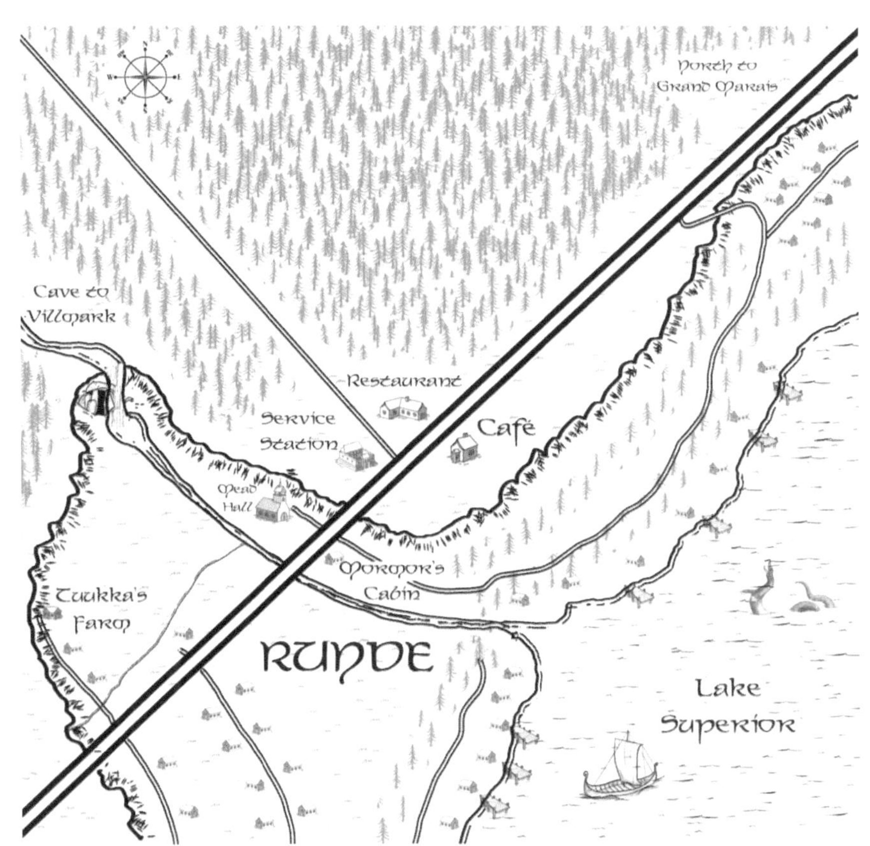

North to
Grand Marais
Cave to
Villmark
Restaurant
Service
Station
Café
Mead
Hall
Mormor's
Cabin
Tuukka's
Farm
RUNDE
Lake
Superior
N
W   E
S

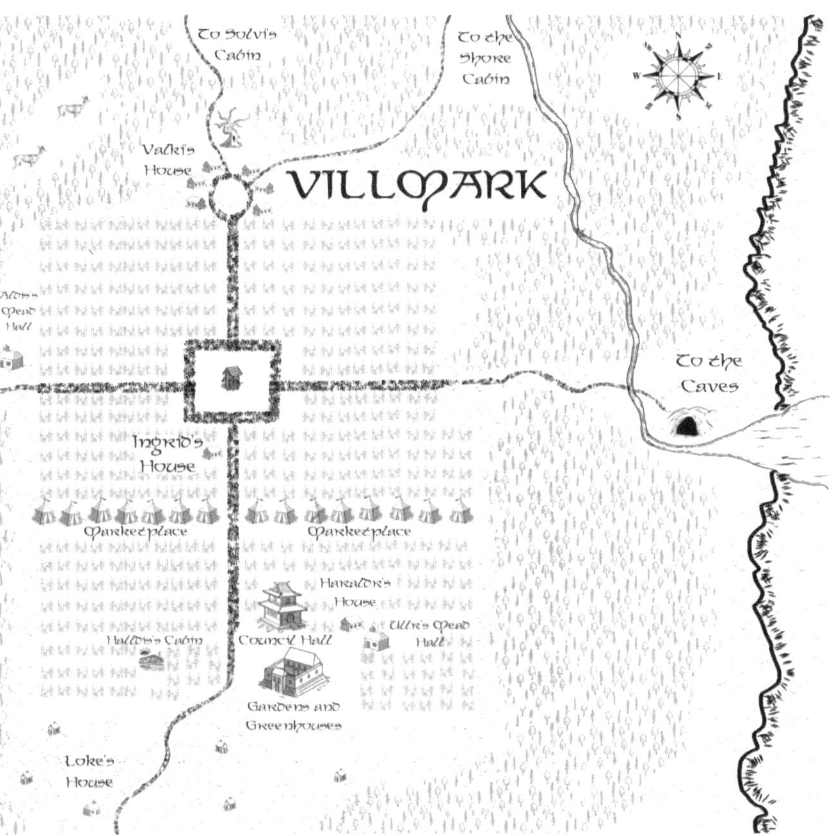

To Solvi's Cabin
To the Shore Cabin
Valki's House
VILLMARK
Alvis' Mead Hall
Ingrid's House
Marketplace
Marketplace
Haraldr's House
Ullr's Mead Hall
Haldor's Cabin
Council Hall
Gardens and Greenhouses
Loke's House
To the Caves
N
S
E
W

CHECK OUT BOOK FOURTEEN!

The Viking Witch will return in **Threat From the North**, available now!

A year ago, Ingrid Torfudottir moved to the North Shore of Lake Superior intending to live a quiet life in the sleepy fishing town she thought her mother was born in. Just her and her grandmother in a snug little cabin, running the local get-together spot while Ingrid pursues a career as a book illustrator.

Instead, she learned that her mother, like her grandmother before her, was born in a hidden village founded in the Viking age by Norse settlers long before the time of Columbus. Ingrid's ancestress wove powerful magic to keep her people safe. And Ingrid wears the mantle of that responsibility now, in the modern age.

She is their volva. Their Viking witch.

But that mantle comes with more responsibility than merely maintaining spells. It means learning all she needs to know, but in half the time any of her ancestors took.

And frequently for Ingrid, it means investigating a murder. Or, in this strangely snowy October, a string of murders. Because when a killer employs magic, no one else stands a chance at stopping them before they strike again.

And something more than unseasonable weather seems to be blowing in from the North.

Threat From the North, the fourteenth book in **The Viking Witch Mystery Series**.

THE WITCHES THREE
COZY MYSTERIES

In case you missed it, check out **Charm School**, the first book in the complete **Witches Three Cozy Mystery Series**!

Amanda Clarke thinks of herself as perfectly ordinary in every way. Just a small-town girl who serves breakfast all day in a little diner nestled next to the highway, nothing but dairy farms for miles around. She fits in there.

But then an old woman she never met dies, and Amanda was named in her will. Now Amanda packs a bag and heads to the big city, to Miss Zenobia Weekes' Charm School for Exceptional Young Ladies. And it's not in just any neighborhood. No, she finds herself on Summit Avenue in St. Paul, a street lined with gorgeous old houses, the former homes of lumber barons, railroad millionaires, even the writer F. Scott Fitzgerald. Why, Amanda can practically hear the jazz music still playing across the decades.

Scratch that. The music really, literally, still plays in the backyard of the charm school. Because the house stretches across time itself. Without a witch to protect this tear in the fabric of the world, anything can spill over. Like music.

Or like murder.

Charm School, the first book in the complete **Witches Three Cozy Mystery Series**!

THE WEAL & WOE BOOKSHOP
WITCH MYSTERIES

In case you missed it, check out **The Teashop Terror**, the first book in the complete **Weal & Woe Bookshop Witch Mystery Series**!

No one knows more about every branch of magic than Tabitha Greene. She devoted years to studying the most esoteric texts, hunting down the most obscure source materials, and deciphering the most cryptic ancient scrolls. But her career in academia hits a dead end when no wizard will take her on as an apprentice.

Just because, despite being descended from two long and prestigious lines of witches, her attempts to actually perform any magic always fail. Often spectacularly.

But no more college means no more dorm life. And no magical skills means no real job skills, at least, not in the witchy world. And a life spent moving from school to school every few months was a life without real friendships. She finds herself alone with nowhere to go.

Then an uncle she barely remembers offers her a summer job, running his bookstore over the summer. The Weal and Woe Bookstore, located in a magical pocket world within a block of buildings just north of the old Mill District of Minneapolis, Minnesota.

Not exactly the pinnacle of all her hopes and dreams. But it's just for one summer, right?

Or so Tabitha tells herself. But unbeknownst to her, the Weal and Woe Bookstore is about to change her life.

The Teashop Terror, the first book in the complete **Weal & Woe Bookshop Witch Mystery Series**!

ALSO FROM RATATOSKR PRESS

The Ritchie and Fitz Sci-Fi Murder Mysteries starts with **Murder on the Intergalactic Railway**.

For Murdina Ritchie, acceptance at the Oymyakon Foreign Service Academy means one last chance at her dream of becoming a diplomat for the Union of Free Worlds. For Shackleton Fitz IV, it represents his last chance not to fail out of military service entirely.

Strange that fate should throw them together now, among the last group of students admitted after the start of the semester. They had once shared the strongest of friendships. But that all ended a long time ago.

But when an insufferable but politically important woman turns up murdered, the two agree to put their differences aside and work together to solve the case.

Because the murderer might strike again. But more importantly, solving a murder would just have to impress the dour colonel who clearly thinks neither of them belong at his academy.

Murder on the Intergalactic Railway, the first book in **The Ritchie**

and Fitz Sci-Fi Murder Mysteries, available everywhere books are
sold.

192

FREE EBOOK!

Like exclusive, free content?

If you'd like to receive "A Collection of Witchy Prequels", a free collection of short story prequels to the Witches Three Cozy Mystery and Viking Witch Mystery series, as well as other free stories throughout the year, go to my website CateMartin.com to subscribe to my newsletter! This eBook is exclusively for newsletter subscribers and will never be sold in stores. Check it out!

ABOUT THE AUTHOR

Cate Martin has written stories which have appeared in **Mystery, Crime and Mayhem** quarterly magazine as well as in the annual **Holiday Spectacular** Advent calendar of Christmas stories. She is also the author of three witch mystery series: **The Witches Three Cozy Mysteries**, and **The Viking Witch Mysteries** and **The Weal and Woe Bookshop Witch Mysteries**. She currently lives in Minneapolis, Minnesota. You can learn more about her work at CateMartin.com.

ALSO BY CATE MARTIN

The Witches Three Cozy Mystery Series

Charm School

Work Like a Charm

Third Time is a Charm

Old World Charm

Charm his Pants Off

Charm Offensive

The Witches Three Cozy Mysteries Books 1-3

The Witches Three Cozy Mysteries Books 4-6

The Viking Witch Mystery Series

Body at the Crossroads

Death Under the Bridge

Murder on the Lake

Killing in the Village Commons

Bloodshed in the Forest

Corpse in the Mead Hall

Slaying on the Lake Shore

Bones by the Forest Road

Sacrifice Behind the Falls

Body Under the Café

Assassination in the Glade

Bewitchment After the Storm

Predator in the Lanes

Threat From the North

Snare in the Blind Alley

Ashes Beneath the Tree (available July 14, 2026 direct from me or August 11, 2026 in stores everywhere)

The Viking Witch Mysteries Books 1-3

The Viking Witch Mysteries Books 4-6

The Viking Witch Mysteries Books 7-9

The Weal & Woe Bookshop Witch Mystery Series

The Teashop Terror

The Salon & Spa Scandal

The Bookseller Blunder

The Entrepreneur Enigma

The Novelty Shop Nightmare

The Courtyard Conundrum

Short Story Collections

Bubbly, Bicycles and Brides

The Dorothy Lundegaard Mysteries

Fruitcake, Festivities and Firelight